THE HERO OF 1000 YEARS

A NOVEL BY

CHRISTINE E. SCHULZE

THE HERO OF 1,000 YEARS
CHRISTINE E. SCHULZE
Copyright © 2012 Christine E. Schulze
Cover Art Copyright © 2012 Christine E. Schulze
Drawings Copyright © 2009-2012 Christine E. Schulze
Edited by Joshua R. Shinn
Formatted by Laura Shinn
ISBN: 9781448689880
Self-Published by: Christine E. Schulze 2012
www.thegoldenhealer.blogspot.com

To Aaron, the Hero.

To Rachel and Hailey for providing many brilliant ideas.

Also to our friends Nathan, Sam, Josh, Krystal, and Tiffany, and our beloved Mrs. Daniels and Mrs. Labrier, as well as everyone else at Berean for being my inspiration.

Be ye angry, and sin not: let not the sun go down upon your wrath.
(Ephesians 4:26)

And be ye kind one to another, tenderhearted, forgiving one another, even as God for Christ's sake hath forgiven you.
(Ephesians 4: 32)

THE HERO OF 1000 YEARS

PROLOGUE

Aaron jumped as one of the large, glass windows swung open wide of its own accord, as though some invisible sprite carried on the wind had reached out and pushed it open. A soft breeze gently fluttered the curtains, carrying a pleading whisper, "Please come...please help me..."

Leaning over the window-sill, Aaron saw a faint light shimmering from the garden far below. The voice seemed to emanate from that direction, and though the voice did not call his name, he felt its tug on his heart; it beckoned him and *only* him. Stepping away from the window, he slipped quickly down the halls, the garden his only purpose, his singular and, for whatever reason, most important focus.

As an unusual white glow illuminated the garden's trees and flowers, Aaron thought the full moon must be uncannily bright that evening—until he stepped into the clearing where the phoenix nest rested.

There, he stumbled to a freezing halt and stared in mingled awe and fear. There, the true source of the light glowed. Between two trees hovered a swirling circle of white light in mid-air. A soft breeze blew from its core.

From deep within, the voice called to him again; only this time, it radiated clearer and more desperate than before, "Please, *please* come...save us..."

Aaron took a few steps towards the portal. Then, as his hand brushed against something cold and soft, he realized his hand was in his pocket. Curiously, he drew out...

The phoenix feather. Its soft, seemingly delicate yet strong fibers wrapped around the emerald green stone he'd used as a prop for his costume. In the game, Hashim had always carried the Emerald of Truth to help guide his steps. He'd started a rogue, but that simple gift had helped him transform into a hero.

With a deep breath, Aaron slipped the treasures back into his pocket. Then, breaking into a run, he plunged towards the portal and leapt inside.

CHAPTER 1

Chasmira, a junior in middle school, felt a little nervous as the carriage approached her new school. Being uprooted in the very midst of the school year didn't help matters either, especially at her age. Magic did not, as normal humans believed, simplify things. It made everything far too complicated—at least in the opinion of a twelve-year old transfer student, such as herself. Twelve was such an awkward age, with emerging hormones, peer pressures, opposite-sex shyness...at least for Chasmira. Not the choice age to leave her comfort zone and start afresh.

Still, despite all these misgivings, the prospect of seeing old friends coupled with the hope of making new friends excited her. The Lynn Lectim Amielian Academy for Fairies and Elves was the largest of its kind in the United States—even the largest in the world—hosting five buildings on campus; an elementary school, a middle school, a high school, a college, and an Amielian chapel. Best of all it was located on beautiful, sunny Hawaii. At least, that's what the non-magical folks had unknowingly dubbed Loz, the largest, most magical, and most ancient of Hawaii's islands.

At any rate, it would prove quite a change from the twenty-student, one-room school house she came from. At that school, all the grades were lumped together, but here she would be a *true* senior—er, no, she would be a true *Celestial*. The ranks of students were named after the old ranks of the Fury thieves, friends of *the* great Lynn Lectim who had founded the school. Thus, the middle school students, as well as the high school students, were named Skylars, Lunars, Solars, and Celestials respectively.

As the carriage rolled through the wooded path, Chasmira enjoyed the clopping of the horses' hooves. Despite technology's many modern conveniences, the school chose to maintain this and other old traditions.

As they rounded a bend, the school buildings loomed into view. Chasmira focused on the old mansion that had stood for over a thousand years, the legendary Willard's Mansion still housing the middle school. Except for a few add-on renovations made some years back, it had remained unchanged all these years. A thrill rippled through her as she considered the deep magic embedded within its walls.

Chasmira's mother also stared wonderingly out the window.

"Isn't it cool?"

Chasmira glanced at her mother. They were both part Scintillate and thus possessed long, straight, flowing, blonde hair that glistened in the sunlight. Chasmira shared the perfect smile her mother flashed at her.

Then, without further reply, Chasmira returned her wondrous gaze to the mansion.

As the carriage rolled to a halt before the mansion's great, stone stairs, Mr. Root, the current principle, a Forest-footer elf with brown hair and bespectacled eyes, hopped cheerily down the steps to greet Chasmira and her mother and to help with Chasmira's suitcases.

"Good morning, Mrs. Eriz, Miss Eriz." He smiled and nodded to each of them in turn, hefting two of the four suitcases.

"Good morning, Mr. Root," greeted Mrs. Eriz. "Sorry we're late."

"That's all right. They've just started math class, but we'll get Chasmira settled, and she can join the English class."

Chasmira smiled brightly. "That would be great." Being spared from suffering through Algebra was the best surprise she could have been offered on her first day.

"I have to go now, honey. I have to catch my flight."

Chasmira turned back to her mom. Tears shone in her eyes, and Chasmira suddenly wanted to cry too, realizing how long she would be parted from her mother for the first time ever.

She hugged her mom close. "I love you. Thanks for everything."

Her mom could only manage, "I love you too," choking on a sob as she squeezed her daughter tightly then jumped back into the carriage.

Mrs. Eriz told the driver she was ready, and as the carriage started back along the trail, she leaned out the window and called, "Do your best! Have fun! Call if you need anything!"

"Don't worry about me! Just have a safe flight! I'll write and call when I can!"

As Chasmira watched the carriage spin out of sight, she prayed her mom would have a safe flight home.

She jumped as Mr. Root jarred her back to reality with, "You ready?" Instantly, her nervous excitement returned. Taking a deep breath, she grabbed the two, remaining suitcases, following him into the mansion.

As they wound through the quiet halls, several staff members nodded, smiling as they passed by in the hallway.

Mr. Root showed Chasmira where the English class was, handed her a map of the school, and then led her to the second floor dorm rooms. Escorting her to her room, he told her to unpack then arrive in the English room by ten o'clock, giving her nearly an hour to settle in.

He then apologized that he must leave so suddenly but said an appointment forced his departure. If she needed any help, she could head down to the teacher's lobby.

As Mr. Root disappeared down the hallway, Chasmira realized with a small frown that the lobby was no where on the map; at least the English room was written in, though in a tiny, almosy illegible scrawl. Perhaps being in such an ancient place *did* have some downfalls.

Walking into her dorm room, she took in her breath. The whole room was so very elegant, with lacy curtains, five canopy beds, two spacious wardrobes, a small table and desk, and a fireplace. All the furniture was rich mahogany and intricately carved, antique along with many other odds and ends. A bathroom had also been added to each dorm room since the house was built.

By the plaque outside the door, Chasmira noticed she shared the room with four other girls—Tiffany, Krystal, Hailey, and Rachel.

After unpacking, Chasmira took the map Mr. Root had handed her, along with a swirly gel pen and notebook, and made her way to English class. It was only 9:45 a.m. and the first hour class was still inside, so she leaned against the wall, patiently waiting.

After a little while, the clomping of footsteps and the onrush of whispering voices flooded her ears. The next moment, the Celestial class rounded the corner, Tiffany, a beautiful Carmella with unmistakable caramel skin and hair, in the lead.

"Tiff!" Chasmira waved.

"Hey, Chasmira," greeted Tiffany as the Celestials stopped in the hallway. "I thought you weren't coming until next week."

"Change in plans."

"That's cool. I see you made it in one piece."

"Yeah, it was a nice ride."

"Figures." Another girl rolled her eyes, flipping her straight, light brown, perfectly layered hair over her shoulders. She carefully reached up to adjust her silver hoop earrings, then smoothed her blouse with a scowl. Chasmira guessed she was a Forest-footer. "*We* always get the carriage with the broken wheel."

"*Or* the stubborn horse," added a girl who was, to Chasmira's utter surprise, even more petite than herself. Her vibrant red hair was pulled back into a pony-tail, and a bandana framed her small, pointed face. Wide-framed glasses framed her bright, blue eyes. Her bell-bottoms covered her feet, and her shirt was several inches too long for her short torso. Necklaces strung with wooden beads and peace symbols dangled from her small neck.

"*Or* we get the carriage with the mule because the stupid horse ran off," smirked a girl sporting a single blonde braid and glasses. Catching a glance at hers and the red-headed girls' green thumbs, Chasmira confirmed her suspicion that they too were Forest-footers.

"*Oh*, the *mule*," groaned Tiff, "I remember that. It took us *two hours* to get to school that day."

"But at least we missed math class," said the brown-haired girl, still scoffing at the wrinkle in her blouse which refused to be tamed.

"True…" agreed Tiffany.

"So, are you new here?" asked the red-headed girl.

"Yeah, I'm Chasmira."

"Oo, coolio name. I'm Rachel. This is Krystal and Hailey—" She nodded to the brown-haired girl and the girl with the blonde braid respectively. "It's nice to meet you."

"You too. I think we all have the same room—"

"Cassy?"

Chasmira smiled as she heard her nickname called in a voice slightly deeper than she last remembered it, yet still warm with its familiar friendship.

She turned.

"Yes?"

"Hello."

Chasmira beamed warmly. Aaron Ruiz strode towards her. His black hair and tall, slim form, as well as his dark, sparkling eyes revealed his father was a

Spanino. His fair skin and the slight, silver glimmer in his hair told his mother was a Velori. He wore a crisp, white shirt and dark jeans, clad simply yet strikingly. His eyes twinkled and his deep dimples showed as he flashed an amazing smile. He looked much the same as he did upon transferring from her elementary school four years ago, except now he stood much taller and had traded glasses for contacts. Like Chasmira, he was also a fairy, though neither of them could fly yet.

His smile broadened a little as he stopped before her. "I didn't know you were coming to school here."

"First day."

Aaron nodded. "Lucky you missed math class—it's a total waste of time."

Chasmira snorted, remembering how Aaron always despised Math.

She suddenly found her eyes straying to a blonde Forest-footer boy with smiley-face stickers stuck all over his face.

"Who's that?"

Aaron glanced over at the boy. "Him? That's Josh White. Hey, Josh, looks like you caught the 'sticken pox' again. What happened?"

Walking over, Josh replied, "Well, my little cousin stuck stickers on herself, and, well, obviously attacked me with happy faces—again. Then Tony dared me to wear them all day to school, but I've already, like, got two marks. Hope I don't get detention—again. Of course, it helps that my sis is out of town, like, so she can't—oh, hello." He suddenly noticed Chasmira. "I'm Josh. And you are…?"

"Chasmira. Chasmira Eriz."

"Nice meeting you."

"You too."

Chasmira looked at her watch. "Umm...does anyone know why we've been standing here so long? Shouldn't class have started by now?"

"*Well*," said Josh, "my older sister usually teaches English, but she's out of town so this is the second week we've had a sub. Not like, a sub sandwich—which by the way we had for lunch yesterday—but, like, a substitute teacher. You'll see why it takes so long. Just wait."

Ten more minutes slipped past in which three people decided to use the bathroom, one girl craved lemonade and returned with an extra-large from the dining common, and Armond, a Limonion boy with bright green hair, drew a game of tic-tac-toe on the wall, landing himself in detention as a teacher passed.

Finally, the classroom door opened, and the Lunars filed out sluggishly, yawning and stretching. The Celestials entered the classroom, taking their alphabetically-arranged seats. Chasmira breathed an elated sigh as Aaron sat in front of her and Tiff behind.

The substitute teacher himself sported a mess of unkempt, blonde hair and crooked glasses, one of the lens cracked. An old tee shirt bore the words "Get free car insurance today!" and old blue jeans appeared as though they might fall apart any second. It was an altogether very unprofessional look, as if he still half-slept, having just crawled from bed.

He droned in a low, drawling voice, "Welcome, class. Turn to page 160—subject/verb agreement. Subject...verb...agreement..." With a snort, his eyelids fluttered, his head dropping onto the desk as he began snoring very loudly.

All around Chasmira, students began writing and passing notes, or rather throwing them, most of them bouncing off people's heads.

"What's going on?" Chasmira ogled in disbelief.

"This happens *all* the time," Rachel, sitting on Chasmira's left, explained.

"It's best just to save English for homework," added Tiffany.

"Or stuff cotton in your ears to keep out the noise." Aaron offered a bit of the fluffy stuff. Chasmira gently declined.

"Doesn't help with getting attacked though." Rachel turned back to her English book as a paper airplane zoomed into her ear.

Mr. Slump, for that was most appropriately his name, remained in his state of slumber for twenty minutes, mumbling things like, "Chicken soup...batteries...caught a big fish...underpants..." With this stately departure, he fell silent.

Overall, the class period stretched as the longest forty-five minutes of Chasmira's life. When 10:45 struck, someone threw a pencil at Mr. Slump's head to awaken him. He was obviously quite used to this treatment, for he promptly mumbled, "Class dismissed."

Hardly anyone heard him make this announcement for all their noise, but as Josh yelled, "*Class dismissed*!" everyone promptly jumped up and filed out, relieved.

As they passed the Skylars, already groaning at the thought of wasting forty-five minutes of their life, Chasmira asked, "So, where do we go next?"

"Ancient Lozolian—our mandatory foreign language," moaned Aaron and another boy with black hair.

"That sounds fun, actually. What's wrong with Lozolian?"

"Well…" Rachel rolled her eyes. "Let's just say Aaron failed his last two tests."

"And *I* got a lowly eighty-three," announced the black-haired boy now walking beside Aaron.

"Wow, such encouragement," muttered Chasmira.

"I got a ninety-eight-point-five," Tiffany announced, staring at the boys with mock-surprise as if she simply couldn't understand how they achieved such crummy grades.

"And me and Hailey both got a ninety-six," quipped Krystal.

Hailey casually twirled her braid. "I mean, the test wasn't *that* difficult."

The other boy sniffed. "For *you* maybe, but Mr. Pero gives us a thousand rules of grammar, a million vocabulary words, then all of a sudden he's like, 'by the way, there's a test next week.' It's *impossible* to remember all that information!"

"Wait." Chasmira frowned skeptically. "The teacher gives you a *week* to study and you *still* can't pass?"

Rachel snorted. "They don't believe in studying any further in advance than two nights before the test. *That's* the problem."

"*Anyhow*," Aaron interrupted loudly, a sign they should change the subject, "Nathan, you haven't met Chasmira yet, have you?"

"Who's Chasmira?" asked the black-haired boy.

"*I* am. Nice to meet you, Nathan."

"Oh. You too."

They reached Lozolian class. Mr. Pero was a much better teacher than Mr. Slump. At least he was awake, which in itself proved a major improvement. He even made a point of welcoming Chasmira on her first day of school. While he covered a lot in the lesson, Chasmira had taken some Ancient Lozolian at her other school and felt glad to discover she wasn't far behind.

After Lozolian class, they all filed into the hall and Aaron announced lunch as the next stop.

"Is the food any good?" asked Chasmira as everyone hurried down the hall towards the dining common.

Aaron smiled with a playful twinkle in his eye. "Let's just say that...lunch is an experience."

Entering the dining common certainly *was* an experience. Madness swirled on all sides—shouting, talking, a variety of smells mixing—and not all of them pleasantly so—while several people accidentally dropped apple sauce and mashed potatoes on each other.

Managing to find the end of the buffet line, the seven teenagers took their positions.

"A bit like rush hour traffic," Chasmira noted.

"Yep," agreed Tiffany, "every day at the same time and everything."

After a few moments, they noticed that the tall boy in front of them wasn't moving. In fact, he stood stock still.

"Umm, excuse me, sir," said Nathan.

Rachel stuck out her neck, trying to peer around him. "What gives, dude? There's no one in front of you for miles.

Krystal sighed irritably. "It's the sleeping dude."

"Who?" asked Chasmira.

"Caleb," groaned Aaron.

Josh smiled proudly. "My brother."

"We call him 'sleeping dude' because the only class he's awake for is Ancient Lozolian. Can't even stay awake for *lunch*." Rachel shook her head as if this notion was both unfathomable and unforgivable. "And the amazing thing is that he graduates *this year*—even though he's a year younger than us, he's a year *ahead*. You'd think he'd be *behind*..."

"Just go around him," sighed Nathan. "We could be here a while otherwise —"

"Whoa, look!" Aaron shouted, pointing.

Their gaze drifted towards what held him suddenly spellbound, and Chasmira gasped. A Carmella boy walked straight up the wall, body perfectly parallel to the floor he'd steadily left behind, eyes closed, lips moving.

"Is he really..?" Chasmira breathed.

"Yup, there's Sleeping Dude Junior," Josh announced.

"That's new," Hailey mused. "He's never sleep-walked on the *wall* before..."

They stared harder as the boy dropped from the ceiling. A girl squealed loudly as he plummeted towards her and as her bowl of chocolate pudding caught his fall. As he blinked, dazed, she glared sharply at him before sauntering off with a harrumph.

"Hmm," mused Aaron, "That *was* interesting—"

"What are you staring at with those muddy eyes of yours? Nothing, perhaps? Maybe Lynn Lectim has adopted a second 'Sleeping Dude,' as the lesser students so creatively dub our dear Caleb over there?"

Aaron groaned, clenching his fists, while everyone else in the group sighed, rolled their eyes, or made some other gesture of annoyance. After glancing uncertainly at Hailey who made a motion between fake gagging and a pirouette, Chasmira turned with the others to gaze at the source of the sudden dread descending upon the atmosphere.

Several feet from them stood a young man about their age. His skin, a snowy white, and his hair, gleaming even snowier, marvelously contrasted against the jet black of the preppy suit he wore. Hands hanging loosely to his sides, the fingers extended like long icicles. In fact, everything about him—arms, legs, body —was long, but not awkwardly so. Rather, an uncanny sleekness clung to him, a strange grace. It was this grace as well as the stark contrast of black and white that made him seem...alluring. Yes, that seemed the right word to Chasmira, the word that summed him up. Alluring. Not handsome, neither cute. Those words didn't quite suit the brooding, snow-white features of his face. But *alluring*, yes. Despite his apparent rudeness, even his abrupt words carried a smoothness, a cunning. And his eyes, soft yet powerful, drew her in by the mere curiosity of their opposite qualities.

Even as he walked towards them, his steps seemed to float. Before he could utter another word though, Tiffany stepped forward, ever so slightly, defensively. Her eyes locked on his, and he froze a moment as if considering. Then, he stormed off, scowling as he glided down the hall.

14

"Scum," Aaron muttered beneath his breath, but Chasmira caught the remark and elbowed him roughly.

"Hey! That's not very nice…"

"Neither is what you just said."

"Trust me," said Rachel, "that's just good ol' Drizzle. He deserves an insult now and then what with all the ones he dishes out."

"Drizzle?"

"Name is Dristann Malloy." Krystal stared at him half-dreamily, half-disgustedly. "Elegant name and a total hottie, but such a jerkface. No wonder he's never had a girl. Worse than this one here…" She jerked her thumb at Josh who stared absent-mindedly at a table teeming with giggling girls.

"Whoa, did someone just point at me?" he asked, jolting back into the conversation.

"Hey, where'd Tiff go?" Chasmira frowned, scanning the crowds. "She was *just* here, staring Dristann down."

"Hm?" Aaron said. "Oh, she always gets ticked off at the mere *mention* of Dristann. Clams up, snaps at us, or just plain leaves."

"Yup," said Hailey, "she disappears randomly from time to time. We think she goes to calm her temperature in the lady's room."

Chasmira searched the crowds for some sign of either Tiffany or the mysterious, snowy stranger, wanting to ask more questions. A growl from her stomach soon reminded her of a more imminent need.

Finally, they reached the beginning of the buffet. Green beans and sprouts were the first delicacy, but as Chasmira reached for the greens, Krystal advised against, whispering, "No one ever eats them, and who knows how old they are, and why does no one ever throw them out…?"

As Tiffany presently returned, looking completely calm, she cut into the line with Krystal. Together they heaped mashed potatoes on their plates, ignoring the irritated snarls of the Skylars behind them, and Tiffany said to Chasmira, "I forgot to mention that Krystal and I have to sit at the teacher's table this week, so we can't eat with you."

"Why?"

"Oh, detention—talking in class." Krystal shrugged nonchalantly as she studied her nails with furrowed brow.

15

"You can eat with me and Hailey," said Rachel.

"Okay." Chasmira turned to Aaron. "And what about you?"

Aaron shrugged. "I'm in trouble as well."

"Shock," muttered Rachel, tapping her foot impatiently as she piled more food onto her plate than Chasmira would have considered possible.

"*You?*" Chasmira stared at him in disbelief. He had always been such a perfect student when she knew him—maybe *too* perfect. "What did *you* do?"

"Well, Mr. Pero said I was talking *again* in class the other day, but it was really Nathan."

"Oh, sure, blame it on *him*," mumbled Rachel.

As Mr. Root called Aaron, Tiffany, and Krystal to the teacher's table, Rachel grabbed Chasmira's arm and began dragging her to a table, Hailey following.

"*Finally*," hissed Rachel. "I can only be nice to him for so long. Do you realize who that annoying creep that's been following us around *all day* was?"

"I—"

"*Aaron Ruiz, my arch-nemesis.*"

Rachel banged her tray down on the table rather roughly and adjusted her bandana with an irritated twitch. Chasmira glanced uncertainly at Hailey who only continued to smile.

"So…why is he your arch-nemesis?"

"Well, you know Nathan, the other black-haired guy you met this morning?"

Glancing up, Chasmira found Nathan still in line, debating between fruit punch and grape juice. He didn't look like any kind of elf Chasmira had ever seen, so she figured he must be a fairy. This was proven when a Forest-footer spilled fruit punch all over the floor and Nathan merely hovered in the air to avoid the drink getting on his shoes. No race of elves could fly, only fairies.

"Nathan used to be my best friend," continued Rachel, "but then he decided to ditch me for Aaron and Sam—" Chasmira followed Rachel's gaze as a Forest-footer boy with curly reddish hair joined Nathan— "Of course, I would be more than glad to make peace with Aaron, but he's always teasing me about what I'm reading, or taking my books and putting them up where I can't reach them, or telling me he doesn't like me with that—that impish grin of his. I mean, I don't

16

mind being teased if it's all in fun, but what really bothers me is that whenever we play four-square, he always tries to hit me in the head with the ball.

"See, I got hit once by someone else, and he says he thinks it would be funny if it happened again. Of course, he's been trying to knock me out since *before* I got hit that time, but whatever. And he's even got *Nathan* against me. Bribed him into hitting me in the face with the ball once."

"Oh. Well, Aaron used to go to my school, you know." Chasmira didn't know how else to reply. Aaron trying to smash a girl in the face with a ball? So bizarre…

"Boy, do I feel sorry for you. And now you have to go to school with him *again*."

"Actually, I'm sure he'd never *really* try to hurt you. He was always so sweet when he went to my school."

"Sweet, huh?" huffed Rachel, taking a big bite out of her turkey sandwich and chomping aggressively. "Yeah, probably when he was *five*. He's annoying now. You'll see after lunch—

"Jeepers! They've just put out the cookies-n-cream cake. That's a rare delicacy around here. Better go grab some before it disappears. Catch you in a minute, peeps!"

As Rachel rushed off, Chasmira stifled a laugh and turned to Hailey, debating on whether she should ask the question tugging with merciless curiosity at her mind. Was it *mean* to ask…?

"Um…Hailey?"

"Yeah?" Hailey intently studied her broccoli, prying apart each tiny stalk with careful preciseness.

Chasmira hesitated again, almost feeling she interrupted some important discovery. But curiosity soon triumphed, and she ventured, "So, um, what's up with Rachel? You know, all the…well…"

"You mean her strangely out-dated lingo, her disregard for modern-day tween slang and wardrobe choices?"

As Hailey continued to dissect her broccoli, Chasmira said slowly, "Well… not that I might have put it so bluntly—"

"It's all right. Rachel knows. She'd explain it herself, but she'll be away at the desert bar a good while, bartering for sufficiently-portioned cake slices. And this broccoli is giving me a fit, so I suppose I can tell you myself…

17

"See, you really can't mind Rachel. She's Forest-footer, yes, but only half. She's also half Cheebite, a race of the eternally young. Not eternally young like fairies—and Scintillates like yourself—who are young forever only in age. Cheebites are also eternally young in spirit, child-like, slow to mature. Explains not only her small size, but also her occasional, random temper tantrums.

"Anyhoo, this is about her third time going through middle school and then high school, and she's always talking about how she's always behind on teen slang and whatnot. Takes her a while to drop old habits and adjust. Hence her current hippy fad and her obsession with all the 'jikes' and 'coolios' and 'jiminy crickets.'"

"Cool-i-*o*! Cake, man!"

Chasmira grinned as she watched Josh return to the detention table with a wide smile, a large slice of cake in tow.

"What's *his* excuse?" she mused.

Hailey shrugged. "He's just Josh. He picks up everyone's bad habits."

She returned her attention to her broccoli, focusing with a menacing, fiery stare upon a fresh stalk. As she began ripping it to shreds as well, she glanced up and said, "I'm going to be an herbologist someday."

After giving Chasmira a very frank stare, as though this fact alone should explain away any of her quirky behaviors, she turned full attention to her broccoli experiment and fell silent.

Thankfully, Rachel slid into her seat moments later, a giant piece of cookies-n-cream cake in tow.

"Score!" she shouted. "Groovy, guys—I totally swiped this from Josh, and made him think he still got the bigger slice…

"Uh…what's Hailey doing…?"

"Herbology experiment," Chasmira said quickly, still imagining the burn of Hailey's eyes. "Um, so let's talk about you. Hailey told me about you being part Cheebite. But why go through school all those times.

Rachel rolled her eyes and shoved a big bite of cake into her mouth. "Well, it was quite the scandal at the time…actually, it's really a good story, *should* be a book someday…

"At the time my folks got together, they were only fifteen. There was this big feud at the time over Cheebites and Forest-footers being allowed to get married and stuff. It was a forbidden romance type of thing on their part.

THE HERO OF 1000 YEARS

"Now all that's finally over and settled, we can stop hiding out and moving all the time. Which means I can finally stop pretending to be as young as I look, finish school once and for all, and be done with it."

"Too...much...talking," growled Hailey who'd lifted two tiny particles of broccoli into her palm and studied them so closely that, had she powers of fire, Chasmira was sure she'd burn a hole straight through her hand.

"Not...conducive...to herbology research..."

Chasmira glanced at Rachel who just rolled her eyes and continued to munch her cake.

After lunch they were granted a half-hour break. Everyone piled into the game room, a massive room where most students gathered to play games, hang out, and, for those who could concentrate past the noise, work on assignments together.

The old ping-pong table that stood since Willard himself dwelt in the house still inhabited the room. As Caleb and a fairy named Tony, as well as Josh, occupied the table and began a heated game, they soon seemed more interested in trying to bounce the ping-pong balls off each others' heads.

A fairy girl with red hair and a blonde Forest-footer sat on the sofas trying to read, but all in vain, for ping-pong balls flew at them every five minutes.

The checker and chess boards with their intricately carved oak and mahoghany pieces were still in use as well. Two Spaninos poured over one of the boards, brows knit deep in concentration.

For Chasmira, it was like stepping into the history book she'd read about this, her favorite room of the mansion. She found it hard to take in all the details, especially as Rachel continued to spout off the names of each random passer-by.

The game room also contained a new addition, a larger, very open area like a gym only smaller and carpeted and used for playing games like dodge ball or four-square. Rachel explained that four-square was the most popular game of choice. Chasmira voiced this seemed a very elementary game, and Rachel admitted this was so, but it carried over as such a favorite from grade school that now only the "uncoolio" students dared to openly mar the name of four-square. And after all, she added, at Lynn Lectim, it could prove a very violent game.

Chasmira determined to watch intently to decipher if it was really worth playing...and soon found herself fascinated. No one played four-square quite like this at her old school. Not only did they play with what was surely the most humongous yoga ball ever made, but the students who already possessed their magic powers soon stirred things up, luring Chasmira's attention.

Things quickly grew interesting as Anyta, an Icean girl whose eyes were truly as sharp as ice, joined the game, accidentally changing Nathan into an ice statue. The most interesting aspect of this was that he managed to stay in the game, since the ball continued to bounce off his head. Eventually, he even got Krystal out. As she could shoot fire, she vented her anger by kindly unthawing him.

Then Rachel and Aaron stepped into the square. Chasmira couldn't help smiling as they bounced the ball back and forth aggressively. However, Aaron hit the huge, yellow sphere so hard that it did truly seem as though he *was* trying to knock Rachel unconscious rather than attempting to get her out of the game, just like she'd said.

Finally, after about five minutes, Krystal yelled, "C'mon, you two. This is *four*-square, not *two*-square!" With a frustrated cry, she shot a stream of fire at the ball, melting it into a shapeless blob.

Everyone groaned as the game came to a sudden halt.

Aaron made a face at Krystal. "Aww, shoot. That's the third one you've destroyed this week."

Chasmira too felt disappointed at not being able to join the game, but she settled with talking to Rachel about the latest books she was reading instead.

After break ended, everyone headed over to history class, taught by Mrs. Labrier, a very elegant Prismatic elf. Chasmira had read much of Prismatics and was humbled to meet such a beautiful lady and have her as a teacher. Prismatics could possess hair any color of the rainbow's spectrum, and Mrs. Labrier's shimmered a soft, sage green, flowing calm and gentle like her eyes. Her cheeks were rosy, and a crown of sage and pink leaves hung about her neck. She wore a crisp, white blouse with an elegantly embroidered collar and a black skirt, simple yet stunning. As she introduced herself and welcomed Chasmira, Chasmira smiled warmly.

As everyone took their seats, Rachel in front of Chasmira, Aaron behind, Tiffany and Hailey on either side, Aaron leaned forward and whispered, "She's the best teacher ever."

"Besides Mrs. Daniels," hissed Rachel.

Since Chasmira had not met Mrs. Daniels, she couldn't contribute to the argument, but she soon agreed that Mrs. Labrier was one of the best teachers she ever had. She actually made history interesting, which was a stunning feat for Chasmira who had never favored the subject. Of course, it might've helped that instead of learning about Lewis and Clark—the teacher at her old school was crazy about them, that was all he ever talked about—they discussed the evil fairy clan known as the Mass, how they were defeated, how the Lectim Academy came to be founded, and how Tristann, niece of Willard, along with the three Wood sisters, ultimately donated Willard's Mansion for the use of the school. Finally, they learned how Amy and Christobel Wood, two of the first students to attend school at the mansion, had saved the school from an enemy who tried to revive the Mass powers. Those two girls, along with Chryselda Sofia the Red, a great queen of old, had then created the Kalvyrie, a group of the most skilled, magical healers in all the world.

At any rate, she proves a much better teacher than Mr. Slump, Chasmira thought, *if you could even call him a teacher.*

Next they all filed to Science where Mrs. White, whose golden, Scintillate curls showed faint hints of silver, greeted Chasmira with a sweet smile.

"That's Mrs. Daniels' mom," whispered Rachel to Chasmira as they took their seats.

Chasmira nodded, thinking that if Mrs. Daniels looked anything like her mother, she must be very exquisite indeed.

"All right, class. Today we shall conduct some star-gazing and learn about the constellations."

The class answered with blank looks and confused faces.

"Umm...Mrs. White?" said Krystal. "It's still day-time."

"Very observant, Krystal," Aaron teased, and several muffled laughs coursed through the room.

Mrs. White continued to smile, undaunted. "Well, it *is* daylight still, Miss Smith. However, we shall be using—"

Mrs. White donned a pair of what appeared to be sunglasses, and everyone was startled when Caleb, who had been sleeping—or at least appearing to be— jumped up shouting, "Anti-glasses! I *love* those things!"

Mrs. White nodded. "Thank you, Mr. White, you may be seated."

Caleb collapsed, only to slip into a deep slumber again.

"Now," continued Mrs. White, "the purpose of anti-glasses is to change the appearance of the sky as you look through them. If I looked out the window right now, I would see a night sky—the stars and moon instead of the sun.

"Who wants to give them a try?"

Almost all at once, everyone popped up from their seats to don the new contraptions. Mrs. White led them outside—Josh all the while boasted how flashy they all looked in their glasses, especially *him*—and handed them each a paper containing names of constellations. Using the guide of their textbooks, they were to locate the constellations in the sky and draw each beneath its name.

Rachel's pencil flew so fast that Aaron warned her to, "Watch out—might catch on fire."

"Why can't *you* catch on fire...?"

Rachel cast him a blazing glare, but her spirits soon brightened as two of the Limonion girls, Glory and Shanika, came asking for help, to which she enthusiastically agreed.

Others though, such as Aaron, Sam, Nathan, and Josh, couldn't seem to find any constellations. Joining together, they decided to chart random stars then connect the dots, hoping they looked realistic. They were having great fun, snickering amusedly amongst themselves, until Mrs. White walked over, inquiring what was so funny. Examining Josh's paper, she just shook her head at the pictures of turtles, unicorns, pizza, and other 'new' constellations. Sensing disaster, Aaron revealed his charming smile. "We can name one after *you* if you like, Mrs. White."

Mrs. White handed the paper back to Josh and walked away, her lips twitching as she stifled a laugh.

The last class of the day was Music. Rachel told Chasmira they took an elective at the end of each day except Wednesday, on which they attended chapel. Tomorrow they would have Art, and on Thursday and Friday they would have P.E. Chasmira muttered irritably that it would prove far more beneficial to attend *Music* two days a week instead of P.E.

Music class was taught by another lady named Mrs. White, more commonly called Mrs. K. White to prevent confusion; she was apparently one of Mrs. White's daughters-in-law.

As Mrs. K. White handed her a music book and announced she was glad she had joined the school, hoping she enjoyed her stay, Chasmira began to feel very at home indeed. Everyone, except Mr. Slump, had welcomed her, and he didn't even really count, being a sub.

The choir was slow to work together, especially as it took the boys a good half hour to review their part, a part Rachel whispered they were to have learned last week. There was also the constant interruption by snores from Caleb, until Mrs. K. White sternly threatened that if he couldn't stay awake, she would find something to keep his eyelids pried open with. This would have sounded harsh, but, Chasmira supposed, he *was* her brother-in-law, not just her student. That granted her certain rights.

Except for a girl singing an octave too high, and a tenor singing totally off key, and yet another tenor who kept trilling his R's, music class flowed quite smoothly.

The last business of the day was supper, doing homework, and hanging out. Krystal and Tiffany decided to meet in the library while Aaron and Rachel insisted on playing four-square. When Chasmira finally grew tired of watching them try to hit each other in the head, she followed Hailey back to their dorm room.

"I'm gonna have to ask for your undivided silence," announced Hailey as she plopped on one of the canopy beds with a huge book. "I wanna get in some study on Egyptian herbs before lights out."

"Okay." Chasmira took a seat at the desk. She wondered what to do for a minute and then took out a piece of paper, a pen, and carefully began to write,

Dear Mom,

What a fascinating day...

After finishing the letter, she prepared for bed, silently thanking Amiel for the blessing to attend such an interesting school and make so many new friends already, inwardly hoping that tomorrow would hold just as much intrigue.

CHAPTER 2

The next day, Aaron proved right about Math class—it literally *was* a waste of time.

Mr. Will would work the same problem over and over again on the board. Oh, sure, a few of the numbers would be different in each problem, but it was still the same problem the whole hour, and the greater issue was he didn't explain *how* to work the problem. So when Nathan tried to raise his hand, Mr. Will kindly told him not to interrupt while he taught class and that Nathan should just pay more attention if he wanted to understand the problems presented.

Chasmira sighed relief as they departed to English class, especially considering Mr. Slump's departure. In Chasmira's opinion, a single day in his class was more than enough torture for one school career.

Chasmira liked Mrs. Daniels at once. Even if the only difference between her and Mr. Slump was that she looked much tidier, Chasmira would've been easily satisfied.

By her golden curls etched with rosy high-lights and fair, flawless skin, Chasmira could tell she was pure Scintillate. But her beautiful, blue-violet eyes could flash stern and powerful if someone forgot their homework or talked in class or chewed gum, all of which seemed to be some of Josh's favorite hobbies. Since Mrs. Daniels was his sister, he delighted in tormenting her, disrupting class using all of the above.

After she had greeted Chasmira, welcoming her to school—Chasmira suddenly realized Mr. Will was the only real teacher who didn't welcome her, though this did not overly surprise or disgruntle her—she asked the class what they learned under Mr. Slump's tutorage.

When no one replied, she repeated the question a bit more ardently. Krystal shyly raised her hand, announcing they had skimmed over the first half of one of the poems, but no one could remember which poem.

Mrs. Daniels shook her head, muttering, "I *knew* he was a mistake..."

Then, to the class, "Well, it appears we're a bit behind, so let's get started. Page ten, please..."

After they finished reading and discussing the poetry, Mrs. Daniels proclaimed their assignment—to write a lyric poem of their own on any subject they wanted.

A few minutes remained before class let out, so everyone took out paper and pen and began composing. Chasmira loved writing and studied her first lines in a pleased sort of way,

"Who flies on wings of silence across the crescent moon,

"Who's hunter during midnight, and takes her naps at noon?"

While Chasmira scribbled about owls, Rachel glared at Aaron whose pen also flew across the page. Then, she stared at her paper, muttering, "What to write, what to write, I *hate* writing poetry...."

Chasmira tensed as a shadow passed over her and a silky voice crooned,

"There was no moon that fateful night,

The stars lay all concealed, save one,

And this thought, fear, into people's hearts did strike:

The work of Silent Death had begun..."

Her eyes scrolled up. Dristann smirked as he towered over Aaron who clenched his pen so tightly his knuckles faded to as ghastly a white as Dristann's skin. Aaron turned his head to glare at him, slowly, as if restraining himself from launching at the snowy figure.

"What's that you have, Mr. Ruiz?" he sneered. "Writing about bunnies again? Is that for your new little girlfriend?"

As his eyes fell upon Chasmira, she blushed profusely beneath the strong pull of his stare.

"Or," his gaze swerved back to Aaron, "perhaps a secret *boy*friend would be more suiting..."

With a growl, Aaron flew from his seat, but in one swift step, Dristann glided back, leaving Aaron to crash hard, sprawling on the rough wooden floor.

"Ruiz, Malloy," Mrs. Daniels hissed sharply, glaring over her half-spectacles as quiet snickers echoed through the room.

With a slight bow, Dristann crooned, "Forgive me, my lady, for my foolish words..."

Mrs. Daniels' mouth gaped just a bit. Even she stood rendered speechless as he slipped back to his seat, a pink flush brushing her cheeks.

"You okay?" Chasmira asked as Aaron scrambled back to his desk.

"Yeah," he muttered, "stupid Drizzle…at least *my* poem's meter isn't sickeningly awful. And I write about rabbits, not bunnies…"

After several more minutes of writing, Chasmira paused and looked up to see Josh carefully folding a paper airplane. She nudged Aaron to get his attention. He nudged Hailey, who nudged Rachel, until all the room was nudged and focused on Josh.

Mrs. Daniels was rapidly writing something at her desk when a paper airplane bounced off her head.

She paused, pinching her lips very tightly together as if stifling a great explosion, then cast Josh such a very sharp look that Chasmira felt extremely relieved she did not throw the airplane herself.

"*Josh*," began Mrs. Daniels.

"Uhh, it was Krystal."

"*Krystal* is in the *very back* of the room."

Josh turned around, spotted Krystal who smiled in impish pleasure, then turned back, mumbling, "Aww, man…"

"Two marks, Josh. Any more, and you will be having lunch with Mr. Root. Everyone back to work, please…"

As everyone turned their attention once again to writing, Rachel sighed, "Ahh, I love sibling rivalry…"

The remainder of the class continued in silence, until right before dismissal when Josh cried, "Ouch! She hurt me…!" in a very high, almost girlish voice.

"What now, Josh?" Mrs. Daniels sighed.

"She slapped me."

"*He* was pulling my hair," Kelsey, a Forest-footer girl snapped.

Mrs. Daniels only smiled. "Well, then, Josh, I'm sure you deserved it."

As Josh stared at her with a look that said he thought Kelsey was worthy of at least twenty marks, Mrs. Daniels cheerily announced, "All right, class dismissed. Have a good afternoon…"

It seemed Kelsey had quite made her day.

* * *

The day passed smoothly, with the exception of Aaron knocking Rachel off her feet with the four-square ball and plunging headlong into a fight with Dristann Malloy as he snickered that Aaron threw the ball like a half-lame girl. Aaron miserably lost the scuffle, especially when Dristann suspended him in the air, rendering him powerless to rejoin either game or fight, cursing all the while beneath his breath his lack of magical skill. Chasmira still hadn't gotten the chance to play, but she kept Aaron's hovering form company anyways.

"It's okay," he murmured. "Just *wait* 'til I receive my powers...."

"Sure you don't wanna play? You have full permission to pummel Drizzle for me...."

"No," she muttered, watching Dristann's sleek, black-clad, snow-white form half-dreamily as did all the other girls clustered about the four-square match. Never had she seen such a crowd. He was such an arrogant, self-centered brat, what on earth drew them all to him so powerfully?

Shaking her head to break from her own trance, she smiled up at Aaron. "What does he have against you, anyways?"

"Dunno," he sighed. "He's hated me from the time he transferred in, first time he laid eyes on me. Bit of a psychotic wack, if you ask me..."

Thankfully, by the time Art rolled around, Dristann released Aaron's bonds, though none too gently. Aaron crashed to the ground, landing half on Chasmira, half on Josh who squealed, "Oww! My ankle!"

Chasmira curiously followed her crowd to Art, intrigued as Tiffany appeared abruptly at her side, announcing that today they would learn to mold clay and create pottery.

The class was taught by Mrs. Enzweiler, a cheerful Washandzee lady. The girls whispered enviously over her gorgeous blue-black curls which trailed her short four-feet frame all the way down to her toes. The boys listened enraptured as she showed them how to work the potter's wheel, gave them some molding tips, and set them to work.

Chasmira soon thought that perhaps the class required more than a ten-minute session as disaster began to quickily creep in.

Sam was trying to mold a bowl that kept turning out as a shapeless blob. Nathan spun the wheel so fast that clay flew about the room; some landed in Krystal's hair and she shrieked in frustration, already too dirty for her liking.

Aaron mumbled to the handle on his tea pot, which wasn't turning out how he wanted, casting occasional, annoyed glances at Rachel who'd already made four perfect little cups ready to be baked.

But the real trouble began when Josh offered Daniel, a Forest-footer with fiery red hair, a cookie containing peanut butter, knowing full well Daniel was allergic to peanuts. This sent him into a sneezing frenzy, and he was promptly excused to the nurse.

As Mrs. Enzweiler was distracted scolding Josh, Caleb slipped over and turned the stove in which Daniel's pot was baking up high. After several minutes, Daniel returned and Josh apologized, though he winked at Caleb at the same time.

After a few more minutes passed, a sudden, loud bang sounded. Everyone jumped in surprise, including Nathan who lost all control of the potter's wheel and clay sputtered everywhere, most of it hitting Caleb and Josh, serving them right as Daniel's pot continued to explode in the oven.

Needless to say, sweet, cheery Mrs. Enzweiler also exploded, telling Josh and Caleb they would clean every inch of the room before leaving class to head to supper.

To the girls' surprise and much to Rachel's displeasure, Nathan, Aaron, and Sam sat at the table right next to theirs that night.

Aaron turned around to tell Rachel, "I wanted to ask you a question about math."

Rachel stared skeptically, suspiciously. "You're asking *me* for help?"

"Why shouldn't I?"

"Because…" Rachel looked on the verge of mentioning something about how he always tried to kill her with the four-square ball, but as Mr. Root stood up, everyone drew silent.

"*Finally*," sighed Nathan, plate overflowing with mashed potatoes. "I'm *starved...*"

"Before we pray and eat," Mr. Root said, "I have an announcement to make."

"Oh, no," groaned Aaron. "This better not be another 'don't throw eggs at the teachers' speech. The last one was a half hour long—"

"Shh!" hissed Rachel.

"As you know," Mr. Root continued, "next week is Fall Break—" A loud onrush of deafening cheers ensued. "—and the following Monday is the annual ball, which always follows our week of Fall vacation."

"Actually, it *usually* follows *Christmas* break," Aaron whispered to Chasmira. "They only changed it last year."

"This year, we're having a special theme. We are to have a costume ball—" He paused as more cheers overwhelmed his voice. "—and you may dress as characters from movies, books, cartoons, video games, whatever, so long as they do not violate any school policies—" He paused to stare at Josh and Caleb as they entered, caked in clay. They glanced about in innocent confusion as everyone stared at them accusingly, as if they'd already jinxed the ball.

Mr. Root vainly tried to stifle a chuckle, turning it into an awkward grunt as he muttered, "All right, then, I will ask for grace and dinner may begin."

As soon as Mr. Root asked the blessing over the food, more talking than eating proceeded.

"This is *so coolio!*" Rachel exclaimed. "Does anyone have any ideas for costumes?"

"I do," said Aaron.

Rachel turned around and glared at him. "You're *not* a part of this. Be quiet."

While he made a face, she stuck her tongue out and swiveled back around.

"Oh, c'mon," quipped Krystal. "We gotta have *some* guys in our group."

"Ooo...fine. But if they cause any trouble, they're out."

Aaron cast the girls a hopeful half-smirk. "So...we're in?"

"Yes," Rachel admitted.

"Yay." He and Nathan hopped over to the girls' table, on either side of Rachel and Chasmira.

"I say we all dress up as giant moose," suggested Hailey with a grin.

"Moose?" echoed Tiff.

"Yeah. Moose are so cool with their huge antlers—"

"No," said Rachel firmly.

"But—"

"*No.*"

"Oh, fine." Hailey wrinkled her nose.

"I say we go with a SpongeBob Squarepants theme," said Aaron.

"Absolutely not," snapped Chasmira. "I can hardly *stand* that ignorant cartoon."

"Really? That's just un-American...not to mention harsh..."

"Your girl's got *some* sense in taste, Ruiz," crooned Dristann, gliding past. "Or rather, *dis*taste. How'd you trick her into being with *you*.?"

He swept out of sight so quickly that Aaron could only glare menacingly at him. A thrill rippled through Chasmira as Aaron at least didn't *deny* her as his girlfriend, and not for the first time that week either.

"Tiff?" said Krystal, and then scowled. "Oh, where'd she disappear to again..."

"Man, he must *really* irritate her," Chasmira said.

"Doesn't he irritate us all?" Aaron muttered.

"Next idea," said Rachel quickly.

Nathan's face contorted into what looked like a very painful knot.

"Nathan?"

"Well, I *was* thinking..."

"Too much thinking can hurt your brain you know," Aaron began, but Rachel elbowed him roughly.

"Well," said Nathan, "we all like video games, right? What if we all dress up as characters from that new game—'Loz: Final Quest?'"

Rachel's mouth flew open. "That is *such* a coolio idea!"

Everyone offered comments of agreement.

"I wanna be Olwen," said Krystal.

"And I'm Zorya," said Tiffany, suddenly popping back at their table, making Chasmira jump and stare in surprise.

"Can I be that one king dude—Hikari?" asked Nathan.

"Sure," said Rachel. "But we need a Chryselda."

"What about *you*?" Nathan asked Rachel.

"Nah, I wanna be Adelyn, the fairy with the neat-o blue hair."

"Isn't she supposed to be *pretty*?" Aaron smirked.

Rachel ignored him and turned to Chasmira. "What about you?"

"Can I be Liv?"

"Sure…but who's gonna be—oh no, we can't let *Aaron* be *Hashim*."

"Why not?" asked Aaron.

"Because," grinned Rachel, "isn't he supposed to be *nice?*"

"Nice one, Rache…"

"Well, I guess that's it then," said Krystal.

"Hey, what about me?" The curly-headed Sam slid in to sit by Nathan.

"Oh, sorry Sam," said Rachel. "Uhh…you can be the other prince dude."

"The one who dies?" Hailey frowned in disapproval. "Well, *that's* friendly of you, Rachel…"

"Oh. Forgot that minor detail. Well, he can be Aiden, the fire sword dude then."

"Ooo, the vampire," Sam agreed. "By the way, Hailey that looks like a most fabulous work on Egyptian herbs. May I?"

"With pleasure…"

As Hailey and Sam began a deep conversation on Egyptian herbs, and as the rest of the group chattered about potential costume ideas, Chasmira's mind wandered as one word stuck out in her mind.

Vampire…

Chasmira's eyes strayed across the room, like instinctive magnets. Dristann stood in the food line. Even the way he held his tray seemed uncommonly grace-ful, his fingers perfectly curled, the plastic perfectly balanced on the tips. She wondered… She'd read of the vampiro curse which had created the first vampire; she read how some were good and didn't prey on human blood. Would they

31

really let such a creature in school, though? She shook her head. Over-active imagination.

Tiffany's head snapped up suddenly, her eyes flaring with dark flames at someone across the room. Following her gaze, Chasmira's eyes drew again to Dristann as he strolled past, his gaze also fiery though still sharply alluring. She watched in mild fascination.

"Yeah," sneered Aaron, "we could have Drizzle join our team and play the part of…a tree? No, too lively. A stone perhaps?"

"Cut it," Tiffany murmured. "Let's just enjoy our food."

Chasmira cautiously peered around, looking for some further sign of him, but he'd vanished yet again. Stomach rumbling, she quickly forgot about the Drizzle, digging deep into her potatoes.

CHAPTER 3

"We're free! Free!"

The first day of Fall Break dawned, beginning one whole week of no studying, no classes, and, in the end, the costume ball.

Excitement abounded, especially from students like Josh who continued sprinting down the hall shouting, "We're free! Free!" until he passed Mrs. Daniels who warned, "I may not be seeing you in my classroom for one week, Mr. White, but that still does not mean I can't give you a mark for running through the hallway." He knocked straight into the water fountain anyway and so decided that if he wanted to run in celebration, it would be safest to go outside.

Also, two Hover-ball games were scheduled during the break, one of which took place that evening, and everyone looked forward to this event, especially Chasmira, who'd never seen a Hover-ball game.

As Chasmira, Rachel, Hailey, Krystal, Tiffany, and Nathan all walked outside together, Chasmira asked, "So...what's Hover-ball?"

"The equivalent of basketball," said Rachel, "only played high in the air. The elves, as well as the fairies who don't have their flying powers yet, wear hoverboots so they can fly. They're really cool shoes—silver with white wings.

"It's kinda lame, really, that it's the only magic sport we have, and it's not really all that magical. Once you get to high school, you can get into sports like mermaide soccer, where you literally get to eat this stuff that makes you temporarily grow mermaid tails, breathe underwater—"

"Hey, Rachel!"

Josh raced towards them.

"Wonder what *he* wants," mumbled Krystal.

He skidded to a stop, panting hard. "Rachel...our coaches want...to talk to us...before the game starts."

"The game's not for *six hours*," groaned Rachel.

"I know, but they're all, like, having some disagreement, and—oh, *no*. Man, where's Aaron?"

"Uhh…"

"He's on our team, and I'm supposed to find him too, and the coach wants me back in five minutes, and—"

"Josh, calm down," said Chasmira. "I think I know where he is. I'll find him and send him to..."

"To the Frisbee Field."

"Right."

"Aww, thanks, Cass." Josh sprinted off in the opposite direction.

"You know, he's a fairy who can already fly...so why didn't he just fly?" said Tiffany.

Nathan rolled his eyes at Tiffany. "It's *Josh*."

"Well, I guess I should go too," said Rachel.

"Okay." Krystal smiled and waved as she rushed off. "Can't wait to see you play."

As Rachel raced after Josh, Hailey asked Chasmira, "So where *is* Aaron?"

"He said he was going to the garden."

"The garden?" echoed Krystal.

"He goes there all the time," said Nathan. "Says he likes to go there and… *think*..." He shuddered as though it was very wrong and dangerous to think too much during Fall Break.

"I'll go find him and meet you guys later," said Chasmira.

"Okay." Hailey nodded. "We'll be in the cafeteria—they're serving ice cream."

Chasmira rushed to the garden, slowing to a walk as she stepped over the threshold into its enchanting spell. She had quickly grown to admire the garden as one of her favorite places on campus. As a soft breeze enveloped her, leading her forward, she gazed about with a familiar wonder at the canopy of thick-knitted trees shading her path. Birds sang quiet symphonies in their distant heights. The very branches themselves seemed to house the garden's own, personal galaxy of stars as thousands of white flowers shone in their winding tendrils above. Rosals whose petals shimmered in a myriad of summery shades lined either side of Chasmira's path. An entourage of scents melded together to add a heavenly touch to the spell which drew her ever deeper, deeper...

34

Until she found Aaron standing in a small clearing where only a single sapling stood, stretching its tiny limbs high towards the sunlight. The clearing was surrounded by a ring of trees, perfectly circular like a crown, or as if all the garden stretching on all sides from the clearing was a legion of guards meant to protect that one, small patch of earth.

Aaron gazed up into one of the trees, a deep concentration glistening in his eyes.

"Aaron?" Chasmira called softly.

"Shh... Over here."

Chasmira tip-toed over to stand beside him, and he pointed up. High in the branches rested an intricately woven nest full of pure golden, phoenix chicks. Their mother perched nearby, watching them with bright, onyx eyes.

"I love this place," Aaron breathed. "It doesn't look like much at first, but then, when you *really look*, there's just so much to see...

"I feel, ever since I came to this garden, I've felt like...like it's going to be a special place for me someday..."

He turned to Chasmira with a half-grin. "Sounds cheesy, I guess."

"No." She scanned the trees thoughtfully as a soft breeze swept across her face, filling her with the fresh aroma of millions of flowers again, making her sink deeper into the dream the garden had already crafted. "No, there's definitely something about this place. About the whole garden, really..."

Something fluttered down from the nest to rest at Chasmira's feet. She picked it up—a phoenix feather. Its edges glistened those of a sharp, golden sword in the sunlight. Tracing her fingers along its edges, she marveled at its soft, delicate touch.

Extending it to Aaron, she said quietly, "They say a phoenix feather is a symbol of everlasting friendship."

He took the feather in his hand and smiled.

"I—I still have those striped paper clips you gave me in third grade," she hesitated, glancing away as her cheeks flushed hotly.

Aaron grinned slyly. "You mean the ones you *stole* from me."

"I didn't *steal* them. I just never returned them." She glanced up with a guilty yet hopeful smile, and he laughed softly.

"Oh," she gasped. "I just remembered. Your coach wants to see you on the Frisbee Field."

"*Now?*"

"Yeah, Josh came looking for you and Rachel."

"Rachel? She's on the opposite team. Why would he want *both* of us?"

"Josh said the coaches were quarreling about something—wait. You and Rachel? On opposite teams? You don't—"

"Try to kill each other?" Aaron smirked. "Nah, but she's a pretty aggressive player."

His gaze returned to the phoenix, but Chasmira's gaze lingered on Aaron; she noted how he played tenderly with the feather before slipping it into his pocket.

Then, Aaron released a deep sigh and said, "Well, I better get going."

"Sure. See you tonight."

"Okay."

Aaron disappeared through the trees, swallowed by the magic of the garden. Chasmira stood awing over the phoenix for a little while longer. Then, casting a final glance at the tiny sapling, she smiled as a sudden, serene happiness washed over her and headed back towards school.

CHAPTER 4

No one was ever sure what the coaches were arguing about, nor why they summoned their teams to the Frisbee Field. A rumor floated about that it had to do with something stupid like a stolen water bottle, but no one could really be certain until they asked the teams after the game that night.

Chasmira, Nathan, Hailey, Krystal, and Tiffany all sat together, about halfway up in the stadium seats encircling the famous—or infamous, Rachel said, depending on what books one read—Frisbee Field. Excited chatter coursed amongst the hundreds gathered, an almost deafening sound which thrilled Chasmira, adding to the heightened exhilaration of her wonderful, first-time experience. As soon as Mr. Root quieted the crowds, prayed, and announced the teams, an even more explosive round of cheers rose up.

Then, the game began.

* * *

Tiffany sidled silently down the corridors of Willard's Mansion. Though most people had already gathered at the game, and though no passersby would see her even if she met any, she always took the chance to practice stealth and silence. It was a part of her job; one never knew when one's powers might fail and natural sneakiness became needed.

Finally stopping before one of the identical doors of the shadowy, silent hallway, she knocked, waiting. Her eyes fell upon the misty light streaming through one of the windows. Grayness clung to the deserted place, a deadness that would've seemed eerie if it wasn't so sad. Not even the distant, muffled cries of the Hover-ball game reached all the way up here.

The softest footsteps thudded, and then the door opened slowly.

"Tiffany." Dristann looked slightly taken aback. "Come in."

She stepped inside, and he secured the door behind them. The room itself was filled with empty, mournful shadows created from the glow of the candles scattered about, illuminating the book spread open on the room's solitary bed. Sinking down on the edge of the bed and examining the book, she looked up and smiled.

"Reading *Loz* yet again, are we? Did I successfully get you hooked after all?"

37

He nodded, casting a small smile her way as he joined her on the edge of the bed.

"The guys don't call you a 'girly wuss,' anymore?"

He scowled. "Doesn't bother me. If *that's* the best insult they come up with...besides, I like Chryselda's story. It's sad, but it ends happily."

"So can *your* story," she whispered, her gaze suddenly full of longing.

He glanced away, sighing deeply. "Can't we endure *one visit* without mentioning that...?"

"Sorry, it's just...you know I *care*, that's all. That's why I came to you before Aaron or Chasmira or any other character. Because you drew me in, because I felt a special compassion for you, wanted to help you, make your story better, like theirs."

"So mine *does* end badly? You admit it?" he growled, biting his lip.

"You *know* I can't tell you anything," she whispered, but her eyes glinted with torture. He needed no further reply. "Last month, a friend of mine...she was helping Drofo from *Ruler of Wings*. She fell in love with him so she warned him of Mullog's treachery, trying to spare him pain. The council whipped her out of there immediately, stripped her of all powers until further notice. Perhaps she'll never travel again."

"Well, at least we don't have to worry about *that* happening with *me*," he muttered. "No chance of anyone falling in love with *this* anytime soon."

Tiffany glanced with a longing hurt in her eyes as his tall, proud shoulders slouched wearily. A great tiredness hung in those dark but beautiful, brooding spheres.

"I wish you wouldn't be so hard on yourself."

"Just as I wish *you* wouldn't always try to act like my counselor. Can't you ever just *be* there, Tiffany?"

She frowned at him, unable to conceal the insult from her gaze. "I *would* be there, if you'd let me more. Maybe then I wouldn't feel the need to scold and counsel every time I see you. You *know* that comes with the territory; this is not my first lifetime, certainly not my first story by any count, so I am not technically thirteen, so if I come off as a scolding adult at times, well, excuse me. But *I* am no more my age than *you* are the age you tell others."

A wry grin lit his face. "Hmm...I suppose that's *one* thing we've in common anyways...

"How are you *here* anyways? You know how much trouble you could get in for being in the boys' corridor...especially with a *boy*," he added with a smirk, as if trying feebly to cheer himself up.

"Have we not just been reminding ourselves of what I *am*?"

"Oh, here comes more scolding..."

"Well, it's your fault this time. You *know* I have powers. Or at least you *ought* to by now. I can make it so that no one can see, hear, taste, smell, or touch me—no one but *you*, if I so choose..."

She glanced up at him hopefully, and for a moment, his eyes lingered on hers, searching powerfully.

She looked away. "Besides, I could ask why *you're* not at the game."

"You should know by now I'm a solitary creature—both by necessity and by choice. I attend the daily rituals of class, meals, childish recess, but beyond that —"

"More by necessity, I think."

Ignoring the comment, he said, "Those hair clips are nice. They suit you."

Glimpsing the elegant painting of the huge, black butterfly hanging over his dresser, she touched the onyx butterflies adorning her ebony hair. "I got them more because they suit *you*..."

"Mmm...so why aren't you at the game?"

"I was. But I knew you'd be here, needing company—I don't need a book scene to know everything. Besides, I don't care much for sports."

He sighed, the dark shadows again masking his fair face. "You're too nice, Tiffany. Too nice to hang around that *Aaron* anyways..."

"Aaron is nice," she retorted defensively.

"Aaron is an arrogant pighead."

"Well..." She couldn't argue. It *was* true, at times.

Dristann nodded, satisfied.

"But must you hate him?" Tiffany pressed. "Must you hate him just because your aunt does?"

"I must hate him because my aunt hates Chasmira, because Aaron associates himself with her, because he is meant to help her..."

"And you are meant to help your aunt."

"Yes."

"But you don't *have* to—"

"Drop it. Please? Can't we just enjoy each other's company like we used to?"

His eyes pleaded, torment shining beyond their mask of spiteful hardness. She couldn't push him further, not today. Besides, deep down, she desired the same thing he did. Just to be together for a time and just *be*.

Nodding, she laid back on the bed, and he did too. For a long while, she watched the orangish light and grey shadows dancing upon the canopy of the bed. Something soothing existed in their flowing, fluid movements, something calming, though the heavy sadness could not be lifted entirely from her heart. Only *he* could take away that burden...

After a while, she turned her head towards him. His eyes were closed as if in sleep, his face peaceful, his tortured eyes veiled, his mind lost in the sweet nothingness of daydreaming. With a slight smile, she sat up, kissed his cheek, and stole silently from the room.

* * *

Rachel quickly proved correct. The game was exactly like basketball, save that the hoops stood hundreds of feet off the ground and everyone zoomed swiftly through the air, and of course there was no dribbling, so traveling was necessarily allowed. At any rate, Chasmira, who'd never been big on sports, felt quite relieved she could understand and enjoy the game.

As the game progressed, the scores remained closely tied. Rachel played on the Sapphire team and Aaron on the Emerald team. As Aaron said, Rachel was a very aggressive—and very skilled—player, but so was he. And the competition between the two was very obvious.

Chasmira couldn't help but smile. Rachel guarded Aaron carefully the whole time, smirking and casting her challenging glares at him. She'd worn her largest, gaudiest peace symbol necklace just for the occasion, and Chasmira wondered if she didn't also wear it as a major distraction and eyesore for rival players.

As Aaron suddenly dropped the ball, Rachel started to laugh, but then she stared.

The silvery glow in his hoverboots flickered then vanished, and Aaron plummeted towards the ground, and Chasmira jumped up with a shriek.

All at once, the crowd rose, straining their necks and eyes to see what was going on, so Chasmira, Nathan, Krystal, and Tiffany couldn't see him hit the ground. Instead, they piled from their seats and frantically made their way down to the Frisbee field, pushing through the hoard of Hover-ball players and coaches flying down to crowd around Aaron.

Chasmira gasped as Aaron clutched his leg, groaning, face scrunched in pain. Then she sighed in relief at seeing he was at least alive, carried on a stretcher by two of the nurses. As they started towards the school, teammates from both teams following, the crowd began to file down to inspect the scene, but Mr. Root's voice commanded over the speakers, "Everyone, please return to the dining common for refreshments. Aaron has broken his leg, but I'm sure he'll be fine. Please proceed in an orderly fashion."

As they all watched Aaron being whisked away, Rachel and Hailey raced up to Chasmira and the others, Rachel exclaiming, "Jiminy cricket! That was the freakiest thing I've ever seen!"

"So, what exactly happened?" Chasmira asked. She rubbed her temple, trying to soothe the sudden pain there and the angst which had caused it.

"Well..." Rachel sighed dramatically, as if preparing for a great spiel. "His hoverboots went out, then he dropped like a cannon ball, and the nurses flew in to catch him, but it was such a long fall, and they weren't expecting it, and he landed at such an angle that they didn't quite catch all of him, and his leg broke."

"Hey, at least he didn't hit the ground and bust his head open," said Krystal with a shrug, carefully removing several cookie crumbs from her silk blouse.

Rachel wanted to laugh, but at a glance at that Nathan, Tiffany, and Chasmira and their anxious expressions, she kept silent.

Hailey quipped in her cheerful tone, "C'mon, let's get some lemonade or something."

They agreed and soon crowded into the dining common where everyone seemed more concerned with talking of the night's events than eating; even Mrs. Enzweiler's famous brownies remained hardly touched.

Finally, as Mr. Root's voice sounded over the speakers, everyone hushed, anxiously listening,

"Mr. Ruiz is going to be fine. Nurse Stevens has prepared her special ivy dust paste, which should heal the leg in a couple days. What Aaron needs now are prayers and encouragement, and rest as well. Let's pray together, and then, if you wish, I will allow some of you to go in small groups to see him for a little while. But after that, we must allow him to rest."

Everyone felt better as they acknowledged that Amiel had watched over Aaron that night and felt even better after trusting Amiel to heal him.

Only five people at a time could visit. Chasmira, Nathan, Rachel, Hailey, and Krystal were first in line to visit Aaron.

Entering the hospital wing, they were surprised and relieved to see Aaron sitting up in bed, sipping what looked like a chocolate shake.

"Hey," greeted Nathan as they gathered around him. "How ya feelin'?"

With a grimace, Aaron set the drink down. "That depends on what you *mean*."

"Your leg hurt a lot?" asked Rachel.

"Oh no, *that's* not the problem. Mrs. Stevens put some green, gloppy stuff on it to ease the pain, wrapped it up, and said the cast could come off in a few days. The catch is I have to drink *this* wretched stuff."

"I thought you loved chocolate," said Chasmira.

"Chocolate, yeah, that's what it *looks* like, but it *tastes* like a mix between peanut butter and tuna."

Krystal's face contorted. "Oh, gag."

"That'd make me wanna upchuck for sure," announced Rachel.

"Yeah." Aaron winced as he took another gulp. "Me too."

They fell silent as Nurse Stevens walked past, then Nathan asked in a low voice, "So, what really happened out there? I mean, with the shoes?"

"Well…" Aaron glanced around, then said, "I overheard the staff talking when I was on the stretcher. Mr. Underwood figures someone tampered with the shoes."

"Who would do such a thing?" asked Hailey.

Chasmira's eyes flashed sharply. "Better not be one of Josh's practical jokes."

Nathan shook his head. "Nah, he wouldn't sink that low."

"Whoever it is, I oughta give them a piece of my mind," growled Rachel.

"Huh?" said Aaron, as he and everyone else stared at her.

"Well, *come on*," Rachel continued, "I was about to take the ball from you, for cryin' out loud."

Aaron rolled his eyes. "Of course, Rachel. Thank you for caring..."

"So, who do *you* think did it, Aaron?" asked Nathan.

"Mutant moose aliens," whispered Hailey dramatically. Nathan snorted, but she glared wickedly at him, her eyes flashing with deadly seriousness. Nathan coughed, almost choking on the suppressed laugh.

"Are we *sure* it wasn't one of Josh's pranks gone mad?" asked Chasmira. "Or Caleb's?"

"No," growled Aaron, eyes flashing with a dark spite. "Malloy...it *must* be Malloy..."

"Malloy?" she echoed skeptically. "He may be a bully, but I don't really think he'd try to *kill* you..."

"You don't *know* him. He *hates* me."

"Aaron—"

"Just drop it, Cassy. Everyone just be warned that if I *even* pass his sniveling face in the hallway..."

CHAPTER 5

All Hover-ball games were postponed until the hoverboots could be properly inspected, but Aaron, Chasmira, and everyone else looked forward to watching the Ultimate Frisbee game being held a couple nights later.

The point of the game was basically to throw an object—in this case, the Frisbee—through the goal, but the difference was that half the players were fly- ers or fairies, and half non-flyers or elves. Since fairies can naturally fly, there was no need to worry about malfunctioning boots, so Frisbee seemed like a fairly safe game.

Thus, only a few short nights after the Hover-ball game and Aaron's "near- death awesomeness," as Josh had taken to calling the experience, the friends made their way to the bleachers.

As they sat back, chattering idly, Rachel dug some little packages of salt from her pocket, ripped them open, and piled salt into her hand, licking it.

"Eww…" Aaron mocked gagging. "Now she's gonna go touch a doorknob or something with her…Rachel spit germs..."

Rachel made a face, sticking her tongue out long.

She then noticed Chasmira staring at her and explained, "We never have salt at my house."

"*Of course* that accredits your weird behavior," muttered Aaron, rolling his eyes.

Mr. Root stood then and began to speak, unknowingly breaking off what would have been another argument between the two. He prayed and asked for Amiel's blessing and safety upon the game, and then it began. The Azurites played against Emeralds, which meant one thing by Aaron's description—they were in for a boring and predictable game. Josh and Caleb were on the Azurite team. They would hog the Frisbee, score loads of goals, knock a few people in the head—this time, Limonions Jarrett and Armond were their chosen victims— and the Azurites would win majorly.

After only five minutes, the Azurites had scored ten goals.

"This game stinks," said Aaron. "I'm gonna get some candy."

As soon as he slipped out of sight, Chasmira whipped out a paper bag and said, "Chocolates, anyone?"

Nathan stared. "You're handing out chocolates—*without* including Aaron."

Chasmira smirked. "Well, I lent him my book and he never *did* return it to me."

As Aaron presently returned, everyone quickly hid their chocolate wrappers.

"Andrew gave me his peppermint drops." Aaron plopped next to Nathan. "No need to go all that way to the concession stands and spend only Amiel-knows-how-long in line since Amiel-also-knows no one will be watching the game—hey, what've *you* been—?"

"Chasmira gave us chocolates."

"What?" Aaron cast her an appalled look. "And you didn't *save* me any?"

"Well, I gave the rest to Rachel, and you know how she is with food."

"Where *is* Rachel?"

"Dunno. She was just here..."

"She liked the chocolates so much that she went to get more," said Hailey.

"Figures," mumbled Aaron.

He popped a peppermint drop in his mouth then immediately sputtered, "Aww, these are *nasty!*"

"No wonder Andrew gave them up," Krystal snickered.

Chasmira tore a piece of paper from the notebook she doodled in, handing it to him.

"Here. Spit it out in this."

"Thanks."

After the Azurites scored two more goals, half-time arrived, and Aaron announced, "I'm gonna get some decent candy. I think I'll buy my own this time."

Not long after he left, Rachel returned carrying an armload of sweets—cotton candy, bags of M&M's, a fruit slushy, and three different kinds of milkshakes.

"Could you hold some of this while I sit down?" She dropped the M&M's in Nathan's lap before plopping beside him.

"You *do* realize you just took Aaron's seat," said Chasmira.

"So?"

"And what's all that stuff?" asked Sam.

"Hmm? Oh, we don't eat a lot of sweets at our house, so I decided to sample a bit of everything—shoot! Forgot the chocolates...

"That reminds me—saw Aaron on my way back. Mr. Underwood, the janitor, was giving him his chocolate-covered peanuts. Maybe I'll nab some from him."

Nathan shook his head. "Some people just can't help themselves...."

As Rachel tore off a gob of cotton candy, plopping it in her mouth, she picked up a crumpled piece of paper and asked, "What's this?"

Nathan, Tiff, Hailey, Sam, Krystal, and Chasmira all cracked up in fits of laughter until Chasmira finally managed, "Umm, Aaron spit in that..."

Rachel threw it to the ground, pretending to gag on her cotton candy.

The game started again, and after about ten minutes, Chasmira frowned. "Shouldn't Aaron be back by now?"

"He probably got lost in the pretzel stand—that happened last month," said Nathan.

"Yeah, maybe…" He *was* rather directionally challenged, or had been in third grade.

Suddenly, Toni, a tall Forest-footer boy, raced up shouting, "Ruiz just *fainted*!"

Chasmira and the others all glanced at each other before springing up and following Toni from the Frisbee field towards the school.

"What happened?" Chasmira asked as they hurried to keep up with Toni's long, quick strides.

"Dunno. Mr. Root reckons it was poison..."

Chasmira bit her lip, blinking back a sudden, annoying rush of tears. Aaron was hurt *again*? *Already*? What was *up*...?

"Chasmira, are you—?"

"I'm fine, Rachel. Come on, let's hurry."

46

They all broke into a sprint towards the school.

* * *

"Aaron?" said Nathan.

"Mr. Ruiz?" said Nurse Stevens.

"He's turning green again—" said Rachel.

"Wait! He's waking up," whispered Chasmira.

As Aaron slowly opened his eyes, his vision blurred at first. Then, as all began to come into focus, he shouted in surprise at the flood of faces staring down at him.

"Yep, he's awake." Rachel nodded, satisfied.

Aaron cried out again as he looked down at his arm. His skin changed from green to blue to pink, the cycle repeating over and over.

"Yes, Mr. Ruiz, you've consumed Sherbert poison. Symptoms include fever, fainting, and your skin changing color," announced Miss Stevens, far too nonchalantly in Aaron's opinion.

"You were out for more than an hour," said Nathan. "We were getting worried."

Rachel added, "Yeah, we thought you might've eaten too much of that stuff. That stuff can *kill* you, ya know. I read about it in this one book—"

"Aww, man! None of your book talk right now," Aaron groaned.

He was quieted by Mrs. Stevens shoving a thermometer in his mouth.

After several seconds, she pulled it out and examined it. "Well, that's good. Fever's down. Why don't you drink some water, Mr. Ruiz?"

Nurse Stevens poured some water and handed it to him. As she walked off, Josh and Caleb barged in, bearing loads of candy.

"Hey, Aaron," Josh began, "we just—"

As Aaron morphed from green to blue, he and Caleb both burst out laughing.

"I'm sorry, dude, but, like, that is just so—"

But what Aaron was, Josh couldn't quite manage to say.

47

When he and Caleb finally composed themselves, Caleb said, "Here. We brought you some get-well chocolates."

As Aaron turned from pink to green again, he moaned, "Oh, please, after those chocolate-covered peanuts, even *I* don't want any chocolate…for a while…did you bring the kind with the caramel—?"

Nathan, Rachel, Chasmira, Sam, Hailey, Tiff, and Krystal all glared at him, and he said, "Fine, you're probably right. I'll lay off for a while."

"So, this is, like, weird," Josh said. "First, you fall from the sky, then Mr. Underwood gives you poisoned candy…"

"He didn't *know* it was poison, Josh," growled Caleb. "If I have to tell you *one more time…*"

"You know," said Rachel thoughtfully, "this is just like this one mystery novel I—"

But as Aaron cast her a warning glance, she drew silent.

Then, he sighed. "Yeah, I *am* getting pretty tired of waking up in this hospital bed with a broken leg or blue skin or—"

He paused, noticing as his skin returned to its normal color.

"Aww, *man*," said Josh. "Well, fun's over. Let's go, Caleb."

"See ya, Aaron." Caleb waved as he and his brother walked out.

Josh's head quickly popped back in the doorway. "Oh, and guess what? We won the game."

"There's a big surprise," muttered Rachel as he left.

"So, umm, any new theories on what's going on?" asked Krystal.

"Malloy, duh, don't need a new theory," Aaron snapped.

"Oh, *come on*, he hates you too much to waste *that* kind of time on you."

"Thanks for that, Krystal, I feel so special…"

"It *is* a bit odd how he's never there for games…or *any*thing involving… *people*…unless it involves *food*…" Nathan's face scrunched into an unpleasant knot of wrinkles again as the wheels turned painfully in his head. "Dunno, the guy likes food but not people. Doesn't seem like such a crazy wack to me…"

While Aaron glared at him menacingly, Chasmira added, "Nathan *is* right, we have no proof. I think you're a bit hard on him at times."

"Oh, so the Drizzle has bewitched you too, ehh—"

"Oh, shut it, Aaron," snapped Rachel. "Just be glad your leg is whole, your skin doesn't look like someone vomited on it, and you have a whole load of candy to devour and thus return that nice sickly pallor to your skin if you so desire."

Aaron sighed. "I just...I worry. I mean, if stuff keeps happening..."

"It'll be okay." Chasmira slid her hand towards his, but she stopped it on his shoulder instead as he stared at the sudden movement. "It'll be okay. The teachers, they'll figure out if something's wrong."

Studying her calming eyes, he slipped his hand into his pocket. The velvet of the phoenix feather comforted him, and somehow, he knew everything *would* be okay.

CHAPTER 6

Monday rolled around again. Everyone was excited about the ball that evening, though not so excited about returning to class.

They did, however, finally get their poems back in English. They had been found in the boys' bathroom, shoved in a crack in the wall. No one dared ask how they got there though Mrs. Daniels eyed Josh and Caleb during the entire class, as if hoping her fiery stare would force them into a confession. This turned out to be a false hope, or else the two boys were actually innocent this time, though the rumor floating around school was that the latter theory wasn't very feasible.

At the end of class, everyone passed their poems around—except for Rachel, who utterly refused to parade hers to anyone. It was the first grade below an A minus she'd ever received. C minus. Not that she didn't deserve it—she viewed it as a terrible poem, worthy of an F.

She crumpled it in her fist, holding it behind her back, as if hoping no one would notice her, but, as Hailey voiced, the smoke spiraling from her ears was quite evident.

"Hey, Rachel," said Aaron, as he, Sam, Nathan, Chasmira, and Hailey all clustered around her. "What's your problem? We haven't heard *your* poem yet."

"Because I can't write poetry worth squat," Rachel snapped.

"Let's see it." Chasmira held out her hand. "It can't be *that* bad."

Reluctantly, Rachel gave it up to Chasmira. As Chasmira read it, her face changed to hold a very conflicted sort of expression, as if she desired to say the poem was at least all right, but as if it really *wasn't*. All she could manage was, "It's…umm…yeah…"

Aaron snatched it, and after scanning it thoroughly, announced, "This is the worst poem I've ever read. Well, besides Josh's…"

Josh paraded around the room, announcing proudly his ability to receive a D minus. Mrs. Daniels shook her head, looking very much as though she wanted to throw a book at his currently fat head to deflate it.

"So, how'd you guys do?" sighed Rachel.

"I got an A minus." Hailey beamed. "Best grade I ever got in English. You wanna see?"

"Sure."

As Rachel read the poem though, she turned crimson. "This is about a *dead fish! How the heck did you get such a good grade when you wrote about a dead fish?*"

"Now, calm down, Rachel," said Sam, grinning proudly at Hailey. "It truly was a phenomenal take on deceased water life."

"Why thank you, Sam. See?" she glared at Rachel. "*Some*one around here can understand the arts...."

Rachel took a deep breath as if preparing to explode back at Hailey, but then Mrs. Daniels dismissed them to lunch.

"Perhaps lunch will fare better than English," Rachel muttered to Chasmira as they hurried down the hallway.

Sadly though, lunch failed. The cook had suddenly taken ill. They were supposed to eat pizza that day, but the replacement cook loved making tuna casserole. In fact, that was *all* she cooked, and as the smell of it flooded the dining common, even Rachel, who normally loved tuna, said the overwhelming stench made her want to upchuck. At this statement, Chasmira cast a very concerned look at Rachel, but Aaron waved his hand, assuring her not to worry about it.

"She's always claiming she'll upchuck," he said. "Right, Nathan?"

"Yeah." Nathan laughed, spraying his tuna sandwich at Hailey. She glared at him very nastily as the chewed-up remnants landed upon her new issue of "Moose, Herbs, and Things: a Well-Rounded Magazine."

"Yeah, Aaron," Nathan repeated, glancing away sheepishly from Hailey, "I remember when you kept talking about that time you ate too much chocolate for Valentine's Day and upchucked all over yourself..."

Chasmira shook her head. "You always *were* a menace with chocolate."

"Hey." Aaron frowned seriously. "If someone sent *you* a 'Barney the Dinosaur' Valentine, you'd be depressed enough to intake a five pound chocolate bar in one sitting as well."

Chasmira shook her head again, releasing a deep sigh, but then she sputtered, "Ugh! That *smell!* I don't blame Rachel, it really *is* upchuck-worthy..."

51

They tried to ignore the smell by talking about the ball and their costumes. As Aaron rambled too much for Rachel's liking about how awesome a Hashim he would make, she stuck her nose in a book.

After lunch, they filed, as ever, towards the game room, Hailey chatting on and on about moose, describing in detail her vision of moose costumes—it wasn't too late to hire a magical seamstress, she assured, to create her vision—when, as they rounded the corner—

"Oh, shoot," muttered Krystal.

Gliding straight towards them, nose absorbed in a thick novel, was Dristann.

"Just keep walking," Chasmira hissed, noting the hardened glare in Aaron's eye, the narrowing of his lips to a thin line.

Her heart raced as they drew closer and closer...

As Dristann slipped past, his shoulder brushed Aaron's ever so slightly, just enough to make him stumble. Aaron froze, fists clenching, then whirled.

"You sneaky, backstabbing. How *dare* you, come face me, you weasel!"

Dristann stopped but did not turn to face Aaron. "I don't think you want to do this, Aaron."

"Come and fight me! If you want me dead, at least face me like a man!"

Dristann whirled, lowering the book, eyes blazing dangerously. "I didn't hex your shoes, fool."

"Don't lie to me! Who else would have the guts—?"

"Talk is cheap, friend," he sneered. "If you want me—"

Aaron rushed forward. Chasmira screamed, clutching at his jacket but he wrenched away, bursting towards Malloy who stood like a proud, still, marble statue, book clutched gracefully in one hand. Just as Aaron reached him—

With a cry, he bounced back as if hitting an invisible barrier, skidding across the floor and crashing into the wall.

"Aaron!" Chasmira shrieked, rushing at him, but Josh held her back. "Naw, man, you don't wanna get involved in this, this is a *man's* duel—"

Blood trickled down Aaron's forehead as he rose to his feet, panting hard, eyes flaring wildly. Still, Dristann stood, eyes dark and cool, stance immovably proud as Aaron surged towards him yet again. And again, he rebounded off some invisible shield, crashing even harder into the wall this time, groaning loudly. He lay panting hard, glaring up at Dristann defiantly. When he made no move to stand, Josh released Chasmira, and she rushed to his side, snarling up at Dristann, "You hateful bully!"

"Bully? *I'm* not the one that throws myself at innocent students. Perhaps that will teach the Late-born to keep his hands—and temper—to himself. Good day, ladies, gentlemen."

Turning, he glided around the corner and out of sight.

"Jerkface," Nathan muttered as he and the others hurried over to Aaron.

"Can you sit up?" asked Sam.

"I think my leg's broken again," Aaron groaned.

"Oh, Aaron," sighed Chasmira.

"Dunderhead," muttered Hailey.

"He was right though," Rachel said, and even as he glared at her, she continued, "Well, you *are* a Late-born, that was just plain *stupid...*"

"What's a Late-born?" asked Chasmira.

"Just means he wasn't born with his powers. Some of us don't get ours 'til we're fourteen or fifteen, you know—"

"Yeah, this is all very enlightening, but, umm, can someone get me up and to the hospital wing?" Aaron groaned.

"Sure thing, buddy," Josh assured, he and Nathan hefting Aaron up. Aaron yelled loudly, cursing beneath his breath, "Gently, guys, gently..."

They all piled up to the hospital wing where Mrs. Stevens met them with a sallow, colorless smile. "Third time this week, Mr. Ruiz? Congratulations on breaking a school record. How may I assist you this time?"

"He thinks he's broken his leg again, Miss Steve," said Nathan.

"Mmm, set him in the bed," she droned, sighing heavily.

As she examined the leg, Aaron squirmed in pain, grunting and glaring disdainfully at the nurse.

Finally straightening, she announced, "Just a minor strain. Fix him up in a minute, hold on..."

As she slid from the room, Chasmira sighed loudly. "Why did you have to, Aaron? He didn't hurt you—"

"No, he only half-poisoned me and—"

"Oh, lay off," Rachel snapped.

Mrs. Stevens returned with a pitcher-full of what looked like chocolate, and Aaron paled as if already consuming the wretched pitcher.

"Where's the green gloop?" Hailey asked.

"Oh, this works into the system faster." The nurse smiled coyly as she handed Aaron the stuff.

"Well, it *does* sort of serve you right," Rachel admitted.

"Is everyone on that jerkface's side?" Aaron quickly chugged the putrid stuff, face contorting as if that caused him way more pain than the leg.

After he finished the liquid, the nurse breezed back in, feeling the leg, and announcing, "Mmm…good as new. You're free to run around, play, throw yourself into any number of other possible dangers, Mr. Ruiz. Looking forward to tomorrow's visit, have a lovely day, all…"

As she swept from the room, Aaron glared after her. "Is she even *allowed* —?"

"Come on, let's go before four-square is all over with," Rachel said.

Taking Aaron's hand, Chasmira helped him from the bed. "You gonna be okay?"

"Yeah, fine," he muttered, following everyone from the room.

* * *

Rachel made her way to the girls' bathroom, glad for a break from the intense four-square game. Aaron seemed to be venting out his anger, playing more violently than usual.

Nathan suddenly rushed past her.

"Hey, Nate, where ya going?"

Nathan skidded to a stop, facing her. He opened his mouth to answer but cringed as an annoying voice called, "Oh, Natty-poo, where are you?"

"It's that Forest-footer girl with the crazy hair—she's after me again."

"I thought she liked Josh."

"She did, but Josh kept ignoring her."

"Josh ignoring a girl? That's a first..."

"Oh, Natty..." the voice loomed closer.

"Well, see you later," said Nathan quickly. "She's been at me *all day* about the ball. She just can't accept the fact that I *refuse* to go with her dressed as a purple bunny with a big, fluffy tail. Well, see ya."

As he slipped out of sight, Lucy loomed into view, nervously ruffling a hand through her wild curls and asking Rachel if she'd seen Nathan.

"He went in the bathroom," Rachel said.

"Oh." Lucy stood right outside the boys' bathroom, smiling dreamily as Rachel continued down the hall, casting her an odd glance.

"You realize she could stand there all day."

"I know." Rachel grinned at Aaron who'd joined her in the hall, momentarily forgetting her great anger towards him. "But it's fun. Once, she stood there three hours and got three days' detention for failure to arrive at classes."

"Are you two actually getting along?" asked Tiffany as she and Krystal approached.

"Umm...no." Aaron snatched Rachel's book and held it high out of reach.

Rachel didn't even try to take it from him, only glared with pure fire in her eyes. "Aaron, *give it back.*"

"Or what?" he laughed.

"That's it, I've been trying to be nice all day, but—"

She stepped hard on his foot and caught the book as it fell from his hand.

"Score!" she cheered triumphantly.

Aaron rubbed his foot, muttering, "Dadgum leg is a death trap, oughta just cut it off..."

Rachel rolled her eyes. "You're such a wimp..."

"So, Tiff," said Aaron. "Where's Hailey and Chasmira?"

Tiff shrugged.

"Thanks for the help."

"I think they're still playing four-square," answered Krystal. "*We* just came down here because we need to go fix our hair."

She flipped her hair dramatically over her shoulder as she and Tiff turned into the bathroom.

Aaron shook his head then cast a mischievous look at Rachel. "See you at four-square, Rachel."

"Yes, you *will*," Rachel promised beneath her breath.

In fact, Rachel played more aggressively than ever. She slammed the ball in Aaron's square, trying to bounce it cleverly in the corners. She used all her tricks but just couldn't get him out. Soon, they turned to the old habit of just trying to hit each other with the ball. The ball flew back and forth furiously between them a full, five minutes.

Everyone laughed as the ball bounced back and forth between the two, but the laughter abruptly ceased and everyone gasped as the ball smacked Rachel directly in the face, making her fall flat on her back.

Chasmira and Hailey both raced to her side as everyone crowded around.

"You okay?" Chasmira asked.

"I think so—" began Rachel, but as she inspected her glasses, her eyes widened in horror. The frames were completely busted in half.

"My mom's gonna *kill* me," Rachel groaned.

"Come on. Let's go find Mr. Root and see what he can do."

As Hailey, Rachel, and Chasmira exited the game room, Chasmira glared at Aaron who stared with mingled disbelief and guilt.

As the girls walked down the hallway, he called after them, "Wait."

The girls froze then turned, Chasmira rigid.

Aaron stood looking forlorn, like someone who'd just lost all his friends even though Nathan stood right beside him.

"Look," Aaron began, "I'm so—"

"Happy?" suggested Chasmira, marching up to him. She was fuming, perhaps even more than Rachel. "Gleeful? Glad? Jumping for joy that you've finally succeeded in knocking Rachel in the face?"

Aaron stepped back, his guilty expression mingling surprise and hurt. "I—I never meant for this to happen, all that stuff I said was just teasing—"

"*Teasing?* It was funny when all you two did was *tease* each other, but it's *not funny* when other people get hurt, Aaron Phillip Ruiz. Rachel is my friend, and she deserves to be treated with the same respect that you treat me with. Rachel was right, you've *changed*. First the crap with Malloy, now this—

"And *you*—" She whirled to face Nathan who jumped, "—she called *you* her best friend, and you take some—some bribe or whatever and hit her in the face too? What kind of friendship is *that*?"

"Look, Cassy—" Aaron began, but Chasmira broke in again, nearly shouting, "*Don't* call me that! And don't talk to me either! In fact, after tonight, don't talk to me at all."

She wheeled around, a bewildered Rachel and Hailey trailing along behind her.

"Chasmira!" Aaron shouted.

But Chasmira didn't hear him. She didn't want to, just as she didn't want to feel the hot, angry tears she fought back.

CHAPTER 7

Finally, the night they'd all been waiting for dawned—the night of the costume ball.

The halls quickly flooded with students sporting some quite interesting themes.

Caleb and Josh showed up as pepperoni and cheese. A Blutonion boy named Antoine was supposed to be the sauce, but he couldn't come up with a costume, so he just wore a red shirt and carried a bottle of ketchup. He fast grew frustrated as no one knew what he was, though several guessed at various, random condiments. Nor did anyone know that Jonathan, his brother, was supposed to be the crust. All he did was carry a loaf of bread around, and everyone assumed him to be a baker.

This upset an Icean girl named Anyta, who *was* actually supposed to be a baker. While she accused Jonathan of stealing her idea, everyone else was busy trying to decipher the little Washandzee Andrew's identity. He was clad in a hideous brown shirt with black buttons down the front, and he wore brown pants with polka-dots of every color of the rainbow. He finally explained that he impersonated a chocolate chip cookie with sprinkles.

While the boys were more interested in dressing as food, as well as eating it, for the party hosted plenty of snacks, the girls took on a more elegant flare. A Forest-footer trio, Kelsey, Kamara, and Erin arrived as Galadriel, Arwen, and Eowyn from *The Lord of the Rings*, while Glory and Shanika both posed as raggedy Ann dolls.

Others of interest included a girl masquerading as a lollipop and Armond's impersonation as toilet paper. He accomplished this by wrapping himself completely in several yards of the stuff, resulting in him barely being able to walk. He took twenty minutes hopping through the food line, and many of those waiting behind him plotted to toilet paper his dorm later that evening.

Chasmira could enjoy none of this humor though. Everyone noticed how she shunned Aaron, and she flushed as red as the crimson silks of her gown, clutching nervously at the emerald pendant about her neck as several passersby stared at her, whispering.

What irritated Chasmira more than anything was that Rachel acted perfectly friendly to Aaron, as though hitting her in the face with a ball every day was a special sort of hobby. In fact, they behaved nicer to each other than ever, and it was making Chasmira angry. True, Mr. Root had been able to temporaily patch her glasses til she could get a new pair. But if Chasmira knew Rachel well enough in the short time she'd had to know her, that shouldn't have been enough to calm Rachel so quickly.

Aaron tried to be nice to Chasmira as well which made her feel slightly guilty, but she was determined to suppress that feeling. *She* had been in the right, not *him*, hadn't she? As he offered a glass of punch, she turned away and replied rather coldly, "I can get some myself."

Thus, the night continued. In fact, Aaron didn't come around her the rest of the night after that cool, shrewd moment. He didn't ask her to play sherades, didn't offer to get her some cake, and didn't ask her to play limbo, though if he did, she might've accepted just to kick him in the shins while they stood in line.

Then again, the limbo floor wasn't the safest place for anyone. Armond discovered that walking under the limbo pole when wrapped in toilet paper isn't the wisest idea. He tripped, knocking into Shanika, who in turn knocked into Glory, who in turn knocked into Keniethia, who in turn knocked into the punch table, sending the punch bowl flying and soaking the three girls. As a result, Armond was forced to hop from the room as Keniethia yelled at him and Glory threatened to strangle him. Shanika followed, mumbling that it was very stupid to set up the punch bowl by the limbo game.

As the mess was being cleaned up so the dance floor could be set up and the girls slipped to their room to change, everyone resorted to playing four-square on the other side of the room—far away from the punch. As Chasmira glanced at the game, scowling at the wretched square and yoga ball, she noticed Aaron wasn't playing. In fact, as she looked more carefully around the room, she didn't see him anywhere.

Rachel suddenly appeared, sitting beside Chasmira who asked, "Where's Aaron?"

"Went for a walk down the hall."

"Oh."

Chasmira continued to watch the others, wishing she could smile and laugh like them. Why should she *care* where Aaron went? It was *his* fault she was in a bad mood, wasn't it? The tinge of guilt returned, but she pushed it away, announcing, "I'm gonna get some more punch. Be right back."

"Okay." Rachel gazed perplexedly after her friend as she scurried off.

* * *

59

Aaron *had* to get out of that room. He couldn't *stand* Chasmira glaring at him every time he looked at her, left with nothing to do but fumble with the green "magic" stone he had placed in his pocket as a prop for his costume. He couldn't bear the constant imagery playing through his mind—Chasmira chucking the stone right at his head like she probably desired to. He wanted to tell her he never meant to hurt Rachel, but she made it entirely clear she wanted him to keep his distance. He wanted to explain how Mr. Root had called them both into his office, making Aaron and Rachel explain all then having Aaron apologize, and then, afterwards, the sort-of friendship he and Rachel had established.

Since she would have none of him though, he could only continue walking down random hallways, thinking and praying about the matter. *Prayer was the best thing anyone could do in a tricky situation*, his grandmother often told him. She was right, and besides, it seemed the only thing he *could* do. Everything had slipped out of his hands, out of his control.

Feeling a little better after all his praying and thinking, Aaron passed Armond hopping around in toilet paper and decided to make a detour to the restroom before returning to the dining common. He turned the corner—

Aaron jumped as one of the large, glass windows swung open wide of its own accord, as though some invisible sprite carried on the wind had reached out and pushed it open. A soft breeze gently fluttered the curtains, carrying a pleading whisper, "Please come...please help me..."

Leaning over the window-sill, Aaron saw a faint light shimmering from the garden far below. The voice seemed to emanate from that direction, and though the voice did not call his name, he felt its tug on his heart; it beckoned him and *only* him. Stepping away from the window, he slipped quickly down the halls, the garden his only purpose, his singular and, for whatever reason, most important focus.

As an unusual white glow illuminated the garden's trees and flowers, Aaron thought the full moon must be uncannily bright that evening—until he stepped into the clearing where the phoenix nest rested.

There, he stumbled to a freezing halt and stared in mingled awe and fear. There, the true source of the light glowed. Between two trees hovered a swirling circle of white light in mid-air. A soft breeze blew from its core.

From deep within, the voice called to him again; only this time, it radiated clearer and more desperate than before, "Please, *please* come...save us..."

Aaron took a few steps towards the portal. Then, as his hand brushed against something cold and soft, he realized his hand was in his pocket. Curiously, he drew out...

60

The phoenix feather. Its soft, seemingly delicate yet strong fibers wrapped around the emerald green stone he'd used as a prop for his costume. In the game, Hashim had always carried the Emerald of Truth to help guide his steps. He'd started a rogue, but that simple gift had helped him transform into a hero.

With a deep breath, Aaron slipped the treasures back into his pocket. Then, breaking into a run, he plunged towards the portal and leapt inside.

* * *

"Hey, Chasmira, it's kinda stuffy in here. Wanna get some air?"

Chasmira wasn't sure if Rachel could read her mind or not, but she felt more than relieved to depart from the sea of staring eyes.

As they walked slowly down the hallway, Rachel asked, "So, what's up?"

Chasmira came to a halt, casting a suspicious glance at her friend and hoping she, of all people, wasn't getting ready to accuse her as well. "What do you mean?"

Rachel paused beside her, rolling her eyes. "Chasmira, you *know* what I mean. You? Aaron? You haven't said two words to him *all night*. At least, not two *nice* words..."

"He's such an idiot!" Chasmira blurted. "What he did to you, and all those other times he knocked you in the head and laughed about it, it's just..."

"Wait." Rachel stared. "Didn't Aaron tell you?"

"Tell me what?"

"Mr. Root called us into his office to discuss the, well, the 'glasses incident.' Anyhow, Aaron said that he didn't know he had been bending my glasses before when he hit me, or how much it hurt when I got hit, and I guess I never really told him either. He explained that all that stuff about not liking me was just teasing, and he didn't mean to make me feel bad, then apologized a bazillion times about my glasses and even offered to pay for them, which I said wasn't necessary, but I accepted his apology, and now we're friends. Well, as close as we'll ever get to it anyways. I'm surprised he didn't tell you..."

"Yeah..." A rotten sort of sickness suddenly churned in her stomach.

"What's wrong, Chasmira? I thought you'd be happy to hear—oh, confound this tape..."

"Yeah, look, I've got to find Aaron. Has anyone seen him?"

Armond hopped around the bend. He was still wrapped in toilet paper but had apparently gotten the hang of jumping everywhere.

"Some guy dressed as a carrot stick said he saw Aaron go towards the gardens."

"I'll be right back." Chasmira sprinted down the hallway.

"Whatever," said Rachel. "I'm gonna go get some cake..."

As Chasmira raced down the hallway, guilt weighed heavily. She finally admitted what she'd been trying to hide the whole night—she was wrong to yell at Aaron, whether he meant to hurt Rachel or not. She didn't even let Aaron explain himself. They had been friends many years and she owed him that much. She had never thought of him as a mean or inconsiderate person. Why was she so quick to judge and speak and not to listen?

All these things swirled in her mind, and she prayed that Aaron would forgive her as she raced so hard her legs ached so that by the time she reached the garden, she stumbled through the trees, gasping for breath. She paused a few moments to catch her breath, then continued her mad search, calling Aaron's name.

But Aaron was nowhere to be seen. Perhaps he had already left the garden, or perhaps he hid, thinking she came to yell at him again. Sinking to the ground, she finally allowed the flood of tears that had been forming all night to spill over.

As she wept, the cool breeze which had sought to comfort her abruptly ceased. The ground beneath her began to tremble and did not stop. With a gasp, Chasmira scrambled to her feet, hurrying towards the mansion. The earth jerked violently, and she made her way through the garden in a zig-zag, falling against trees for support.

As she exited the garden and came to the mansion, she stumbled and fell hard against the stone steps. She took in a sharp breath as pain shot through her side.

The next instant, that pain faded, replaced by an unearthly cold as a darkness passed over her, a darkness like a shadow and yet deeper than that of a mere shadow. Slowly, she lifted her gaze to stare upon the black figure looming in the doorway.

CHAPTER 8

Rachel met Nathan in the hallway.

"Okay," Nathan drew a deep breath, "this is freaky. I can't find Aaron *anywhere*."

"And I can't find Chasmira." Rachel's lips were drawn into a grave line; worry flashed vividly in her eyes.

Looking up, they noticed Hailey, Krystal, and Tiffany striding down the hall towards them.

"Hey, where'd you guys go?" asked Hailey.

"We're looking for Aaron and Chasmira," said Rachel. "Can't find them anywhere."

"We didn't check the attic," suggested Nathan.

"We're not *allowed* in the attic," reminded Tiff.

"And that would stop Aaron?" snorted Krystal.

"What about Chasmira?" asked Rachel. "It's not like her to break school rules..."

"Look," said Nathan. "They couldn't have just vanished. Let's check everywhere again."

After thoroughly searching the upper levels, they met again in the third floor library.

Rachel frowned. "Now, I'm worried."

"Shouldn't we tell Mr. Root or something?" asked Hailey.

"I don't know. I mean, where could they have—?"

The mansion suddenly jerked as though an enormous beast rammed into it, and they braced themselves against the tables and shelves.

"Whoa," breathed Nathan. "What was *that?*"

"Something weird..." Tiff glanced about nervously.

"This *whole day* is weird," said Rachel. "First, people disappear, then—"

Another, more violent tremor gripped the building, and Mr. Root's voice announced over the speakers,

"We appear to be having some kind of earthquake. Everyone proceed to the main floor as soon as possible—"

The entire building quaked again, and Krystal screamed as a bookshelf nearly toppled on top of her. Tiffany veered out of the way of a crashing lamp.

"Let's get out of here!" commanded Nathan, and none dared disobey.

The building shuddered again then began to sway, almost rhythmically as if dancing. Walls and bits of ceiling began to cave and crumble about them as they scurried down the hall, then the stairs.

Finally, they reached the entrance hall where everyone else began to crowd.

More an abrupt moment, things grew very calm.

Then, another jolt shook the mansion, followed by the gently swaying motion. This time, the mansion's eerie waltz did not cease.

"Okay," breathed Krystal. "Now I'm *really* freaked out."

"Don't worry, everyone." Mr. Root strode into their midst. "We're just going to make our way outside—" As he swung the door open, he nearly tumbled out, then quickly shut it. When he turned to face the students and staff, his face had blanced pale with fright.

Casting Mrs. Daniels and several other teachers a worried look, they replied with their own, uneasy glances.

"Everyone remain calm," Mr. Root called above the murmuring crowds, "Please sit while the teachers and I go out and investigate what is happening."

As Mr. Root departed the room, the other teachers and staff following, he commanded the teachers who were elves to take hover boots with them. Everyone else sat on the floor, whispering and mumbling.

"What do you think's going on?" asked Nathan.

"Dunno." Tiffany shook her head. "You think it's got to do with Aaron—like a plan to take over the world or something?"

Rachel stared at her. "*Aaron? Take over the world?* I know we're worried, but let's not be stupid—"

"I don't mean *Aaron's* taking over the world," snapped Tiffany. "I mean, maybe he knows something and he's gone to stop whoever's causing this mess. Or maybe he got captured when he was in the garden, or—"

"Clouds!" Krystal interjected. She stood gazing out the window.

"Yes, those *are* clouds," Nathan said.

"No, I think she means that just a minute ago, we could only see trees outside the window," Tiffany said. "You know, we're kinda surrounded by a forest and stuff…"

"Where you going?" asked Nathan as Rachel headed to the window. "We're all supposed to stay seated."

"Since when have *you* ever followed rules since hanging out with Aaron…?"

Rachel made her way to the window, cautiously stepping over students and treading slowly as the mansion continued to dance as if caught in a gentle wave.

Then, bracing herself, she peered out the window. When she turned back toward the others, her face showed complete disbelief.

"We're floating."

"What?" asked a nearby boy, his face flooded with panic.

"We're rising—the mansion, that is," Rachel announced, raising her voice. "We're no longer on the ground."

Students rose and crowded in droves around the windows, gasping and muttering.

"What do you think it all means?" asked Krystal, as she, Nathan, Hailey, and Tiff pushed their way through the masses to where Rachel stood.

"Looks like a pretty good 'take over the world' plan to me," mused Tiffany.

"This isn't funny anymore," Rachel muttered solemnly, gazing out the window. "It's not funny at all…"

CHAPTER 9

As the bright light faded, Aaron fell flat on his back, hitting his head with a thud.

He sat up rubbing his head and finding himself in an attic crowded with piles of antiques. It was dark except for a stream of sunlight filtering through a tall, glass window.

Beyond the window, beside an old chest, crouched a girl with long, dark, wavy hair and midnight blue eyes which stared right at him in shock.

"Who are you?" she breathed. "And where did you just come from?"

"I'm Aaron—Aaron Ruiz—and I came from the Lynn Lectim school, but who are *you?* And where the heck *am* I?"

"In the Lynn Lectim school. But I have never seen you here before. I am Alyssa Liv, though I am known to most as Liv, Liv of the Mira elves, a student here.

"Oh, dear," she cried softly. "You're hurt."

"What?"

"Your head—it's bleeding."

Reaching up and touching his head, blood stained his fingertips.

"It's all right." He shrugged. It was only his fourth accident in a period spanning less than one week.

"No, let me help," she urged, drawing a white handkerchief from her sleeve.

A strange feeling washed over Aaron as she rose, stepping from the shadows into the white light streaming from the tall glass window. A golden halo of light encircled her pretty head, and Aaron felt very humbled, as if he stood in the presence of a great princess or even a queen.

Then she stepped out of the sunlight, shrinking back to a small, thin, yet still very beautiful young maid.

After gently wiping the blood that trickled down the side of his head, she applied pressure to the wound.

"Thanks…"

His gaze trailed to her gown of red and white, simple yet elegant and very similar to the one Chasmira wore to the ball. Something prompted him to ask, "What year is this?"

"1005."

She did not sound surprised by the question. Her mind seemed to wander afar off, and he noted the sadness shimmering in her eyes.

She released the pressure on the wound. "There, that should do. I'll take you to the hospital wing and have it bound properly."

Liv started towards the door, but Aaron said, "Wait," and she stopped, turning back towards him.

"Is something wrong?"

"Umm…I'm not from around here."

"Oh, that's all right, I'm sure Miss Lynn won't mind a guest—"

"No, I mean—" He took a deep breath; the very idea seemed so absurd— "I'm from the future."

"What?" she whispered, staring at him.

"Where I live, it's over a thousand years from now." He quickly explained about the voice, the portal, and how he came to be there.

"That was *me*," Liv breathed in awe. "You heard me talking to myself, only…I must've summoned you by accident—no, not by accident. Amiel answered my prayers…"

"Your prayers?" Aaron echoed, even more perplexed.

Liv gazed off distantly again, the sad expression veiling her features once more.

"Is something wrong?" Aaron asked softly.

"No, nothing." She quickly turned to him again. "My troubles are not important right now. We must get you to Dr. Cassidy."

Aaron followed her from the room. A bizarre sort of de-ja-vu came over him as he walked down the same corridors he'd headed down only moments ago and thought about how he was really one thousand years before that time. Everything looked strikingly similar, even some of the people. They passed a girl whose hair was as red as fire, a girl with a blonde braid, and another with light brown hair—*perhaps they were ancestors of Rachel, Hailey, and Krystal,* he mused.

As the girl with red hair called out, "Hey, Liv, where'd you find *him*? He's a cutie," he immediately doubted her connection to Rachel. Still, as the girl with brown hair flipped her shiny locks over her shoulder, he felt certain she, at least, could be related to Krystal.

Liv led him up a familiar flight of stairs to the hospital wing where Dr. Cassidy rushed to greet them.

"Thank Amiel someone else is here," the doctor muttered. "I *had* to get away from that incessant sneezing."

"Danielle got into walnuts again?" asked Liv.

"Yes. The Whitley twins' doing, probably. And who have we here?"

"Aaron Ruiz. He's taken a nasty fall and hurt his head."

"Well, let me take a look..."

As Dr. Cassidy led Aaron to one of the beds, Aaron heard someone sneezing repeatedly in a nearby room and resisted a smile, remembering one of Josh's and Caleb's more recent pranks.

"Have a seat, Mr. Ruiz."

Aaron sat on the edge of the bed. Dr. Cassidy examined his head, cleaned the wound, and bandaged it much more carefully than Nurse Steve might have done.

"Not too bad," assured the doctor. "Why don't you rest a spell?"

Aaron slipped beneath the covers, suddenly realizing his great tiredness. Though only late afternoon here, night had been closing in when he left his own time.

Liv bid him farewell, promising she would visit him later. After muttering a sleepy thanks to her, Aaron entered a dreamless sleep, slumbering on through the night.

* * *

As bright, warm sunshine streamed over Aaron, he opened his eyes. With a yawn and lazy stretch, he snuggled further beneath the soft covers, preparing to close his eyes again, when something moved in the bright light of the window, and he glanced up.

Someone seated on the window seat turned their head towards him. Blinking in the bright light, he sat up a little. The person started towards him, and when no longer drowned in the white light, a young woman stood before him, tall, fair curls of strawberry blonde sweeping over her shoulders. Long, white robes swept the floor. The sunlight touched her body with the same majestic aura he'd felt upon Liv, and he sat up straighter, trying to tame what he knew was wild bed-head.

The woman's eyes shone deep and thoughtful, as one who has lived many years and witnessed many things, yet a youthfulness clung to her appearance. *She must be a great fairy*, he thought.

She eased gently onto the edge of his bed. "Aaron, do you know who I am?"

A strange question, he thought at first. How could he know someone who had lived one thousand years before his time? Yet, a familiarity clung to her wisened, girlish features. Perhaps they learned of her in history...

"I am Lynn—"

Aaron's mouth flew open, and he stared. The great Lynn Lectim was talking to *him!*

She laughed softly at his expression "—and Liv tells me you are Aaron Ruiz from a time a thousand years in Loz's future."

Aaron nodded. He couldn't speak, shock stealing the words away.

"I believe Amiel has sent you here for a purpose," she continued. "An evil force has entered our world. You are our last hope in this dark hour..."

Aaron continued to stare, now in confusion.

"Has Liv not told you of our troubles?" Lynn asked.

"No, ma'am."

"I see...well, I shall leave that for her to explain, when she is ready."

"May—may I go see her now?"

"Yes, if you are feeling up to it."

"Yes, ma'am, my head feels a lot better."

Lynn nodded. "Then I give you my leave. I think you will find her in the stables."

She arose, but before leaving, looked him straight in the eye. "Remember to trust in our great Lord Amiel, for He will never fail you. May Amiel bless your mission."

She left Aaron to think upon her words for some time. What *had* brought him here? And why had Liv denied anything was wrong when he could clearly tell something troubled her?

In silent pensiveness, he walked to the stables. Thankfully, their location didn't change in the past thousand years; he still knew exactly where to go.

Upon entering the stable, Aaron halted. Liv stroked the nose of a white horse, sobbing softly.

Unsure whether he should leave or say something, he debated a bit before venturing, "Umm...you okay?"

Liv looked up. She smiled, but no happiness touched her eyes which sparkled with tears.

A deep sigh escaped her. "This morning, I told you nothing was wrong. That was a lie..."

Turning her gaze back to the horse, she continued to stroke it gently. "Several months ago, my parents died, and since they were teaching me, I had to come here. My friends don't really understand. *No* one understands how I feel...and now I'm going home for the Fall break, and my cousins are all off visiting their relatives, and I feel so...alone..."

The last word slipped from her lips so faintly, like a thin vapor destined to fade.

Hugging the horse's neck, she wept.

Aaron shifted awkwardly, wondering what to do. Walking over, he presented a tissue from his pocket, extending and offering gently, "Here."

She stared at the tissue blankly.

"Uhh...it's a tissue—kinda like a modern-day handkerchief."

Liv accepted it, smiling, her eyes expressing the gratitude which her tears did not allow her to utter.

After a time, she found her voice, whispering, "Perhaps you are the answer to more than one of my prayers."

"What? But how can I help—?"

"Not here." Her gaze darted about the stable, suddenly flickering fear. "You never know when there may be spies around. We will speak of it later..."

"Hullo, Liv," chirped a man's cheerful voice. A rather gruff, plump, though jolly-looking man sauntered into the stable. He wore a tattered cape over his worn tunic and looked as though he could've used a good shaving, but his eyes danced warmly.

"Stillman." Liv brightened a bit at his presence. "I want you to meet Aaron."

Stillman tipped his balding head in Aaron's direction.

"Stillman here is my horse-tender, also my escort. He'll be leading us to the Mira Woods tomorrow."

"Nice to meet you, sir," greeted Aaron.

Stillman simply nodded and smiled.

"They's gettin' ready for breakfast."

"Then we should get back. Thank you, Stillman. Come on, Aaron."

As Aaron followed her back to the mansion, she slipped her hand in his. As she graced him with a hopeful smile, something warm lit his heart. Perhaps he would find purpose here after all.

CHAPTER 10

The following dawn, they departed for the Mira Woods. Stillman led them, riding a brown horse, Liv upon a white mare, while Aaron had borrowed a gray horse from Lynn. As they slowly trotted off into the woods, Aaron took one, last glance at the mansion. How beautiful it was, and just as mysterious as the first time he'd beheld it in his own time, canopied by lush, green trees, wrapped in endless ivy tendrils. On the balcony, Lynn stood and waved to him, eyes blazing with a powerful hope and a reminder of her wise advice. Then, in the blink of an eye, she vanished.

For many hours, their journey stretched silently. Aaron had already surmised that Stillman was a man of few words, communicating mostly in nods and smiles.

Liv's silence, however, was not one of shyness, but of sadness, of brooding worry pooling clearly in her eyes.

The intense quiet finally pressed in too heavily, and Aaron decided to talk about his own time. Liv listened silently, though not without interest in her distracted gaze, about all the modern advances in transportation, music, communication, medicine, though Aaron quite failed to explain what a video game was.

Stillman looked quite intrigued as Aaron talked about hamburgers, french fries and voiced he might like to try a "Whopper" some day.

Aaron then talked about his friends and how things ran at school. Liv laughed what seemed to Aaron a long-forgotten and much-needed laugh as he told her of Josh's antics. A bit of sparkle returned to her eyes, more than satisfying him.

He then spoke of Nathan, Sam, and Rachel. But upon reaching Chasmira, he hesitated, and then quickly started talking about Whoppers again. He and Chasmira did not end on a good note, and guilt pressed against his heart, especially as he wondered if he would ever see his time again, ever reach her to apologize...

By nightfall, Live and Stillman at least were in a far more pleasant mood than when the journey began. They camped beneath a lofty tree, and Stillman even said, "G'night, Aaron," before going to sleep.

"Good night, Stillman. Good night, Liv."

"Good night, Aaron," Liv whispered, casting him a smile that made him blush deeply.

Stillman and Liv drifted to sleep, but Aaron remained awake. He was to keep the first watch. For a while, his thoughts and prayers kept him busy. But as the warmth of the fire filled him, a sleepiness flooded him also, and, slowly, his eyelids closed.

* * *

When Aaron awoke, it was early morning. Stillman already sat on his horse as Liv cooked some bacon Lynn had given them. Aaron thought it odd that Stillman should miss breakfast when he had consumed three times as much as he and Liv for supper the previous night, obviously a man who enjoyed his food. Now, however, he sat on his horse, cloak wrapped tightly over his shoulders, hood shielding his face. Perhaps he wasn't a morning person and could actually sleep up there. He *did* keep the latest watch. Or perhaps he was just eager to get going. Either way, they couldn't know, as he'd already fallen into his familiar silence.

After breakfast, they packed up their blankets and delved into the woods once more. Their journey was to last two more days, and Aaron looked forward to them.

The day started well enough. Liv seemed a lot happier than the first day he met her, and they talked some. But as the day progressed, silence descended once more.

Aaron was beginning to wonder about their guide as he led them deeper and deeper into the woods. He hadn't removed his cloak or hood all day, his face remaining shrouded in its folds. Starnge, considering how humbly cheering he seemed yesterday. Aaron shook his head. Perhaps his own sleepiness caused his imagination to run wild, accusing Stillman where he had no cause.

Yet, as he glanced at Liv, concern glistened in her eyes as well.

Finally, she prompted, "Stillman, this isn't the way we usually come. We're supposed to stay near the main path."

Silence. Not even a nod.

"Stillman?"

Stillman paused. Finally, he would turn them around. But, no. He scanned the trees and bushes as if waiting for something.

Then he nodded his head, and four archers leapt from the trees, surrounding them, arrows set to the black strings of their ebony bows. They dressed in black from head to toe and stood poised, glaring menacingly.

"Stillman..."

Liv stared in horror as the man lowered his hood. It was not Stillman but another of the shadowy men clad in black.

The Stillman impersonator nodded his head towards them, and the archers raised their bows.

"Let's go!" Aaron shouted, tugging at the reins of Liv's horse. At first, she sat frozen in shock and horror, then she led her horse into a gallop alongside Aaron's.

They fled until the archers disappeared from sight, but the echo of thundering hooves soon approached as the archers pursued on steeds of their own, their bows and sharp eyes still bent with a single purpose—to take down Aaron and Liv.

Liv ducked as an arrow soared over her head, but the next moment, her horse fell beneath her. She tumbled to the ground, stunned. Her horse lay whinnying in pain, dark blood staining the ground beneath it. She knelt, patting the faithful beast's side hesitantly, but there was no time to tend to the horse. Reaching up, she grabbed Aaron's outreached hand, swinging herself upon the horse behind him.

"Thank you," she breathed.

"No problem, but I think you better thank me later. How close are they?"

Liv turned and cried, "Duck!" as an arrow headed straight for their heads. "Pretty close."

"Boy, we could use a Flashling about now."

"That gives me an idea. I summon Taylor, my Guardian Fairy!"

A tiny, white, glowing form shot from beneath Liv's tight curls. She sported two golden wings, two purplish-bluish braids, and a pink, long-sleeved tunic with bell purple pants, both clothes and hair adorned with flowers and raindrop-shaped crystals.

"Guardian Fairy at your service!" she chimed.

"Taylor, how's your levitation coming?"

"Hmm...well, sometimes it works, and sometimes it doesn't."

"It'll have to do. Help us over the cliff when we get to it."

"Okay."

"Aaron, turn to your left."

Aaron pulled the reins and the horse veered to the left, the archers following suit.

Taylor turned her interest to Aaron. "And who is this?"

"Hi, I'm Aaron. It's nice to meet you—" He ducked to avoid a branch. It was hard to see with a fairy hovering right in your face.

Taylor sighed, staring at him dreamily. "Ooo, it's nice to meet *you* too..."

Another arrow zipped past, narrowly missing Liv's ear, and she cried, "Taylor, please, not now!"

"Oops, sorry, mistress—"

"Uhh, we're kinda approaching a problem here," noted Aaron. They exited the woods, speeding towards the edge of a cliff.

"It's all right," assured Liv in a soft but determined voice, "just keep going."

This seemed an insane command, but only two choices lay before them—plummet off a cliff to their doom, or get shot full of arrows. Neither appealed to Aaron, but then he remembered Lynn's words, "trust in Amiel," so he prayed...

As they leapt off the edge of the cliff, his prayers were answered. Taylor shot a glittering dust which enshrouded the horse's hooves, floating them to the cliff beyond the ravine. The black archers brought their horses to a halt, powerless to do naught but stare in amazed disgust.

Aaron led the horse into the woods, silently thanking Amiel for their delivery, then slid off the horse's back, helping Liv down. They both sat on the ground, exhausted from the excitement.

Aaron suddenly realized his swiftly reverberating heart. "Who were *they?*"

"The black archers." Liv's face was both solemn and white with fear. "They've been following me—they will follow *you* now too." Her eyes flashed up to meet his.

"But...why? Why us? We're just kids. What could we have that they want?"

"Remember how I said I was praying for someone to come? I was praying for someone to save me and my people, and then Amiel sent you.

"There is a dark lord, Rorrim, whom we call the Dark Master. He comes from a time and place different from our own, seeking the power of the Destiny Stones.

75

"Before the great fairy Zephyr died, she made two prophecies, one to me, and the other to Zorya, daughter of Chryselda Sofia.

"Both spoke of great evils approaching, and now the first is upon us.

"Rorrim wishes to use the Destiny Stones to banish all who oppose him into the past, into the dark land from whence he came. With everyone who is against him out of his way, he can take over Iridescence, and eventually, the whole world.

"The prophecy spoke of three who would hold the three stones in their hands —the Princess of Destiny Past, the Princess of Destiny Future, and the Hero of 1,000 Years.

"Zephyr has told me I am the Princess of Destiny Past, and you, Aaron—" Her eyes met his, flashing with all seriousness. "—can be none other than the Hero of 1,000 years, the Hero of Destiny."

"And...then, who is the Princess of Destiny Future?" Aaron asked slowly, trying to grasp the shocking reality of all she shared.

"That, I do not know. Zephyr said she would be a descendant of mine. Therefore, she must be either part Mira or Scintillate, for I am a Mira, and my people and the Scintillate people are very closely related. The same blood flows through our veins—the same youthful appearance remains with us for life..."

As Liv's voice trailed, Aaron thought of Chasmira. She was *at least* part Scintillate and very beautiful. He wondered if she could be a descendant of Liv, and she would certainly make an appropriate princess.

But Liv broke into his thoughts as she stood to her feet. "I wonder what has become of Stillman. I hate to think what they might've done to him. But we cannot search for him now, only pray and hope for his safety. Come. We must get going."

Aaron helped her back on the horse then swung himself on.

"Travel west," Liv commanded, drawing silent afterward.

She directed him until they emerged from the woods. Aaron stopped the horse as they stood on the brink of a wide, open space.

"Labrier's Glen," Liv declared.

Aaron gazed at the wide expanse, an eerie chill rippling through his body despite the warm, afternoon air surrounding him. It was too open, too unprotected.

"Is this the only way?"

"No, but it's the fastest." He sensed a hesitance in her voice and eyes. But speed *was* what they needed.

They galloped across the clearing, his heart racing just a little faster with each step, as if its acceleration could spur the horse's hooves to race yet faster.

As they reached the middle, a horn blew, and Aaron brought the steed to a halt.

"What's that?"

"Its sound is unknown to me," Liv breathed, and Aaron felt her arms tighten around his waist.

Aaron glanced all around the field. There was no one in sight.

Then the horn sounded again, suddenly very close, and from the woods behind them surged no less than two dozen men dressed in black, galloping at full speed to encircle them. They looked like the black archers, only they bore swords sharper than the deadly arrows.

"Let's get going!" Aaron shouted, nudging the horse who didn't need to be told twice.

But as fast as their horse fled, she was tired still from their last run, and the warriors quickly neared.

"Taylor!" cried Liv. The little fairy napping on her shoulder darted up, wide awake.

"Taylor, ward off the black warriors."

"Yes, my lady!" she piped.

Giving Aaron a broad smile and a wink, she soared off behind them.

Aaron glanced over Liv's shoulder. Taylor was tiny but mighty. She hurled balls of white light at the archers, knocking several off their horses.

After only a couple minutes though, she returned, fluttering up to Liv, panting, "There are too many. I knocked a few down, but more are coming, and my power's sapped."

The black warriors streamed out of the woods on every side, the hooves of their massive, black steeds thundering powerfully.

Aaron and Liv were surrounded on every side. The black warriors all stopped, and Aaron stopped their horse as well. There was no use in taxing the poor horse further when outrunning their foe was now a clear impossibility. As one of the warriors shouted a command, they all drew curved swords of a dark silver.

"Draw your weapon, Aaron!" Liv cried. Fear flooded her eyes, face, every inch of her expression.

"My weapon?" Aaron echoed. Fear crept inside his heart too as he watched the warriors closing in on them, blades of malice thrust high, spearing the air; Aaron imagined those blades spearing his body, and that of Liv's...

"*Draw your weapon*," Liv repeated, voice trembling.

He reached behind him and took Liv's hand. He thought of Chasmira.

"Dear Amiel," he breathed, "help me protect her..."

Even as he muttered the words, his hand trailed to something hanging at his side. The sword from his costume! It was only plastic, but he drew it.

"*That's* your weapon?" Liv ogled the pathetic blade. "Taylor, go help him if you've enough power left."

Taylor sprung into action, soon transforming Aaron's sword into a real one.

"Liv," said Aaron. "Get down and take cover."

Liv leapt from the horse and crawled beside a small boulder. It was hardly a hiding place but might offer some protection from the myriad of blades meant almost solely for her flesh.

The first onrush of warriors met him. Taylor obviously had fused some magic in the sword because he hit his every target, the blade glowing triumphantly each time. Taylor meanwhile thumped the warriors on their heads, shouting, "Take that, you great bullies!"

A scream rent the stormy sky like lightning. One of the warriors yanked Liv onto his horse. Sliding off his own horse, Aaron rushed to her aid, but she managed to kick the fiend and he fell to the ground, stunned.

As the battled waged on, more and more warriors appeared and in greater number, some on foot and some on horseback, all making Aaron grow tired. There were too many for him to handle, and no magic could keep his strength uo for long.

Hearing a shout behind him, he turned, only for a blow to land sharply on his head. As he stumbled to the ground, another pierced his side. It was the most incredible pain he'd ever felt, yet he did not cry out. He could make no noise, and his vision grew fuzzy before he blacked out...

Whimpering in horror, Liv rushed to his side. A nasty bruise formed on his head while blood gushed from a wound in his side.

Feeling a cold shadow pass over her, she looked up. As the warrior who injured Aaron stood before her, she did not look upon him with fear but with an intense fierceness. As he swung his sword downward to claim Aaron's life, Liv snatched up Aaron's sword, blocking the attack. She had lost so much already, she would not lose him too, he who proved such a true friend when she needed one most. She struggled against the warrior, but he disarmed her, but she did not panic. Sinking to the ground calmly, she prayed, ready and eager even to accept death, if it had come to that. She wished only that Aaron could somehoe be spared...

The warrior lifted his sword to slay her—

There suddenly burst a great gust of light, a noise like thunder, and the warriors cowered to the ground. Liv looked up and saw a great fairy in hovering above them. She was not one of the tiny fairies like Taylor but stood taller than any woman Liv had ever seen. Her long, sage green hair wisped about her fair face like flowers' soft fingers, and she bore a crown of sage and mauve leaves. Her dress was simple, plain and of an earthy color, yet a sense of power, wisdom, almost majesty flowed from its glowing folds.

She was youthful in appearance, except her eyes which were not aged in many years but in much wisdom. Deep, sharp eyes bearing the most piercing look Liv ever beheld. She bore also a white scepter, from which emanated crackling, jagged fingers like white lightning. As the warriors again drew nigh, swords drawn, she pointed the staff at them, and bolts of white light shot in every direction, knocking them off their feet or tumbling off horses.

Liv then noticed another figure standing beside the fairy. It looked like an over-sized rabbit, only it bore a sword and attacked with lightning-fast strokes.

She watched in amazement as the terrible team threw down the black warriors in great numbers, lightning bolts flashing in all directions. Those who could retreat did so to the woods while those who could not escape fell, instantly motionless. Just as abruptly as it started, the battle ended, and all drew silent.

Aaron had lain, rendered unconscious, unable to see anything for some moments, but now, as he opened his eyes, he saw Liv standing over him, her gaze fearful. His first thought was that the enemy still pursued them, and he tried to spring up to defend her but couldn't move. The next eyes he saw were a soft green, calming sage spheres that made him realize his intense tiredness.

His vision faded in and out...in...and out...then faded altogether.

CHAPTER 11

Slowly, Aaron awoke. As his senses gradually stirred, he noticed several things. He lay on his back, on something soft and squishy. He rode in a sort of cart or wagon—it was very bumpy. All he could see above him were branches of trees covered in the reddest leaves, interspersed with patches of blue sky and sunlight. The leaves calmly fluttered down around him, kissing his cheeks as if welcoming him back to the realm of consciousness. The pain from his wounds seemed to be entirely dissipated.

He sat up.

"Oh, Aaron—look, Labrier, he's awakened." The voice was Liv's. She sat right beside him in the wagon.

"Ahh, finally," drifted another lady's voice. The wagon was driven by the green-eyed fairy and pulled by a black horse. Aaron's eyes lighted upon a white mark on the horse's flank, a patch of fur shaped like a lightning bolt.

"We were worried a while, but Labrier was able to heal your wounds. Thank Amiel she was there," said Liv.

"Yes," announced the green-haired lady. "Fortunately for you, I was not far from my glen."

She turned to face him. "It is nice to meet you, Aaron. I am Labrier."

Aaron nodded. It was all he could do as he sat rendered speechless again. Not only did she *look* much like Mrs. Labrier, his history teacher, she also shared her name.

Must be an ancestor...

He looked about at the red-leaved trees that seemingly stretched on forever. The leaves appeared to be constantly falling—the wagon was covered with them —yet the trees teemed with leaves, no matter how many fell.

"Where are we?"

"The Mira Woods," said Liv.

"The leaves are constantly growing and falling," explained Labrier. "It is said they possess healing powers. I suppose *you're* proof that's true. I used them on your wounds..."

81

"Thanks," said Aaron. "For saving us, that is."

"You're welcome. Though I *did* have a little bit of help."

"A little?" As the creature who spoke stepped from behind Liv, Aaron stared. He was like an over-sized rabbit, save that he bore a sword tied in its sheath about his waist.

"*A little?*" he repeated irritably. "*I* was the one who had to fetch the awful, scratchy leaves—not *at all* to a bunny's liking. This whole place makes me sneeze. I wonder if I shouldn't keel over breathing in the scent of these nasty leaves—" He lunged into a sneezing fit.

Labrier cast him a sharp glance. "Calm yourself, Twitchy. Aaron, this is Miramar Twitchy, my sidekick, you might say in your time."

"Nice to meet you." Aaron held out his hand.

Miramar did not shake it, though. He sniffed it then turned away. "Well, it wasn't nice meeting *you*. *You* were conked out and *I* had to fight all those nasty warrior men—"

"Hush, Twitchy," said Labrier, and then to Aaron, "Look. The Vale of the Mira is upon us."

As they stepped up over a ridge, Aaron gazed down a long, smooth hill at the bottom of which stood the most glorious city constructed of trees—trees thicker and taller even than the tree of Malachitess. The Mira had carved out rooms within the trees and elegant doors and windows in their sides, and tree houses and shops nestled in the far-stretching, lofty branches. All the trees were connected by sturdy bridges swaying gently in the wind. The city was protected by a thick wall of trees closely knitted together. A glorious, golden gate was set in the wall, two lookout towers flanking it.

Labrier stopped the wagon at the top of the hill, turning to Liv and Aaron.

"This is where I leave you."

"Thank you, Labrier."

"Yeah, thanks," added Aaron, hopping out and helping Liv down.

"You are both welcome."

As Labrier turned the wagon around, they heard Twitchy ranting, rather loudly, as if primarily for their benefit, "Oh, sure, no one thank the poor bunny who did all the work—"

"Thanks, Twitchy!" Aaron called, though he wasn't sure the bunny could hear him over all his complaining.

Aaron followed Liv down the hill and up to the gate. In the midst of the gate was painted a giant, red leaf, the crest of the Mira.

Liv knocked three times.

"Who goes there?" boomed a voice from one of the high towers.

"Do you not recognize me, Captain?"

"Of course, my lady! But who is he that travels with you? Be he friend or fiend?"

"Friend, Captain. He has come to help us in our time of need. Already has he saved my life. Though it is also beyond me why I should purposely bring a fiend into our midst."

"Of course, my lady. Well, then, I should like to meet him."

A Mira man leapt from the tower, and Aaron jumped as he landed agilely on his feet, right in from of them.

"I am Haliv, Captain of the guard." He extended his hand.

Aaron shook it. "I am Aaron Ruiz."

"Nice to meet you, sir. We are honored to have you here in our time of need.

"Open the gate, men!"

As the golden gates swung slowly open, Haliv led the way inside, declaring, "Make way! The princess has returned, bringing with her an honored guest, Aaron Ruiz, a great hero!"

Aaron wanted to hide behind Liv as everyone both in the trees and down below stopped to stare at him, his cheeks flushing as vivid a burning red as he had seen Chasmira's do on multiple occasions.

But his focus soon concentrated on Liv. As Haliv led them beneath the lofty trees and all the buildings housed in them, he brought them to a short though very wide staircase, at the top of which stood the three largest, thickest trees Aaron had ever beheld. They were pure white, connected by bridges carved with elegant swirls and shimmering like moonbeams. The middle and front-most tree could only be entered by a pearly white gate, and Aaron guessed this must be the palace. As the gate swung open, a great light poured from it, illuminating Liv, casting upon her dark curls a bright, golden, contrasting glow. Like starlight shining through the darkest night. In fact, her whole being seemed to glow from within, and he suddenly realized why she possessed such a majestic air upon their first meeting—she truly *was* a princess, destined to someday become a queen. He stood staring at her, thinking all these things, when her fluid voice caused him to snap out of his reverie.

"Aaron, Aaron, aren't you coming?"

"Uhh...yes." He sprinted up the stairs, walking through the gate with her as Haliv led on.

They entered a hall and before them rose great double doors, but they didn't pass through these, instead departing through a small door. Inside, a staircase wound upward. This they climbed and at the crest slipped through another door and found themselves on one of the outside bridges. Haliv led them to one of the adjoining trees and finally to a room handsomely furnished.

"Will you find these lodgings comfortable?" Haliv asked.

"I should hope so." Aaron stared in amazement at the tapestries, silk curtains and bedding, wonderfully crafted furniture, and cozy fireplace.

"Is there anything else I can do for you or your guest, my lady?"

"No, Haliv, thank you. That shall be all."

"Yes, my lady. Should you need anything, you know where to find me."

As Haliv bowed and left, Liv turned to Aaron. "I am going to my chambers to rest. Dinner will be served shortly."

She turned to leave, and then turned back. "Aaron, thank you again."

As she smiled sweetly, Aaron returned a grin before entering his room.

Liv fell fast asleep by the time dinner arrived, and upon receiving this message, Aaron took his meal into his room then retired to bed. As he lay among all the soft pillows though, he did not fall asleep right away, instead pondering over the happenings of their journey.

As he recalled Lynn's words, "You are our last hope in this dark hour," he slowly began to fathom the importance of his mission. Silently, he thanked Amiel for bringing him here, for keeping him safe thus far, and asked Him to help him complete his destiny and truly become worthy of his title as the Hero of 1,000 Years, whatever that that might come to mean.

CHAPTER 12

Aaron woke early in the morning to someone shaking him. Opening his eyes, Liv's wide, blue spheres gazed down at him.

"Come," she whispered. "I must show you something."

He followed her outside. The sun was just rising. How beautiful she looked in her pale, pink robes, like a spring flower. The soft sunlight glinting with golden hues upon her dark brown curls. A serene quiet settled over all, and Aaron guessed they were two of the only people risen as of yet.

He followed her behind the palace, through a cluster of thick trees with no homes lodged in them. As she stopped, he halted behind her.

They had reached a wall formed of thickly entwined vines and branches. Liv unlocked the pale, golden gate which swung slowly open, and they stepped inside.

As they tread down a flight of stone steps, huge hedge walls loomed up on either side so Aaron could not see where they were going, but he guessed they had just entered a garden.

At the foot of the steps rose the thick, solid trunk of a tree seemingly forming a dead end. But Liv tapped the wood in a rhythmic sort of pattern, and as a doorway opened, they passed through to the other side.

They stood in the garden now, blossoming trees, flowers, and cool, clear pools of water encompassing them, yet this garden was like none Aaron ever saw before. Scattered all about were circles of emanating, white light, like the same portal he had passed through from the garden at school to the attic where he met Liv.

"These," said Liv quietly, "are the portals of time and space. There are many such portals throughout the world, but this garden holds one of only two portals that can return you to your time. Come..."

She led him through the garden until the trees became so closely knit they could hardly squeeze through. Finally, they stepped into a small clearing barely large enough for them to both stand in. A round, wooden door hovered in their midst. Pictures of cars, planes, all sorts of modern things were carved upon its surface, and Aaron wondered at their accuracy and at who could have carved it.

"This is your door. The most carefully guarded in all this garden. But it is locked, and only Amanda Danielle holds the Destiny stone that may open it. All three Destint stones may open worlds, but the Hero's is the most powerful, and only by it may you return to your time. You must see Amanda Danielle as soon as possible, for the sooner you receive your stone, the sooner you can figure out how to defeat Rorrim."

"Who is Amanda Danielle?"

"A great fairy, the wisest in these lands besides Labrier. She too owns a garden, three days' journey from here. You must go there."

"But...when?"

"Tomorrow."

"*Tomorrow?*" He had been hoping to spend more time exploring here and especially to get to know Liv a little better.

Liv took his hand, gazing with a deep seriousness into his eyes. "Aaron, I am not sure exactly what your mission is, but you are the hero Amiel has chosen to save us. Therefore, you must depart as soon as possible."

"But what about you?" Aaron protested. "Don't you want me to stay here 'til next week—til you go back to school?"

Liv smiled. But it was not the same, sorrow-stricken smile he had painfully witnessed so many times. A light had returned to her eyes, a gleam of hope.

"The sooner you go, the sooner Rorrim will be defeated, and we can put all this behind us.

"I appreciate you keeping me company though, for lifting my spirits. You're a good friend, Aaron."

As she said this, his gaze shifted to the ground. A twinge of guilt stung his heart.

"Something is bothering *you* as well. I've seen it these past days."

Aaron sighed. "I'm not such a good friend as you think. There are two girls at my school, Rachel and Chasmira. I was kinda mean to Rachel, I mean, not on purpose, but, well, it turned out disastrous, and I broke her glasses. Then Chasmira and I got into a fight because she thought I did it on purpose, and I apologized to Rachel. But Chasmira...I don't know if she'll ever talk to me...and I've been wondering why Amiel would pick *me* to be the hero..."

"We cannot understand all Amiel's ways or reasons, but I believe it is because you have a righteous and pure heart. And what is important is not why, but that Amiel has appointed this task to you—no one else can do it."

He smiled a little, though he couldn't help but still doubt her words.

"As for Chasmira, were you two good friends?"

"Well, sure, I guess—"

"Then do not worry. If she is as true a friend as you claim, I'm sure she's forgiven you already. She's probably worried about you right now. And Amiel does not want us to dwell on our guilt but confess our wrongs, and He will forgive us."

Liv smiled warmly, and Aaron grinned in return.

"You're right. Thanks. You'll make a great queen someday."

Liv blushed profusely, her gaze darting away. "Well, now that's all settled, all that's left is to appoint you a guide—someone who knows the woods and can take you directly to Amanda Danielle's garden.

"Taylor!"

Taylor shot from beneath Liv's curls.

"Taylor, guardian fairy at your service!" she giggled brightly.

"Taylor, will you please go get Dianne?"

"Right away!"

Taylor disappeared and returned with another, tiny, glowing fairy at her side. She sported short, wind-tossed, fiery red hair, golden wings, a dress and tights of purple, blue, and green, and little green boots. Golden beads adorned her hair, and around her neck, a leaf pendant. Her bright, blue eyes glowed with sharp criticism.

"Dianne, I'd like you to meet Aaron, Hero of 1,000 years—he's come to help us."

Dianne scanned Aaron before snorting. "*This* is the hero? I thought the hero should at *least* be strong or handsome..."

Aaron turned to Liv and whispered, "Is she the only available fairy?"

"Yes."

"I can't have Taylor?"

"Sorry," replied Liv, and her eyes sparkled mischievously. "But Taylor is *my* guardian fairy."

Aaron sighed deeply, resigning himself to a long and arduous journey as Dianne continued to glare, squinting disapprovingly.

* * *

"Have you read, 'Why Do Cats Hate Water?'"

"No," drawled the unenthusiastic reply.

"Have you read, 'History of Anicleo?'"

"No."

"Have you read, 'Of Flowers and Herbs?'"

"No..."

They were on the third and, thankfully, *last* day of their journey to Amanda Danielle's garden, having not met with any danger. *Her constant talking probably scares any enemies or wild animals off,* thought Aaron with a scowl.

Each day, Dianne contrived some new device with which to entertain herself and annoy Aaron at the same time. She had been prattling about books for the last half hour. It was like having Rachel constantly buzzing about his head. He tried throwing rocks at her, but of course, she was too swift and would dart out of the way then sneak up behind him and pull a hair from his head, giggling mischievously as she pocketed it like some twisted trophy.

She was asking, "Have you read, 'Battle of Hasty?'" when he decided that maybe if he said "yes," she would fall quiet. Yet when he did, she began asking him what his favorite character was, what his favorite part was, what he thought of this or that, and when he replied he couldn't remember to each inquiry, she simply said, "Boy, you sure don't have a good memory," and returned to spouting off her list of favorite books. Of course, Aaron realized, though disdainfully, that she *was* his guide, so he really couldn't do anything about it.

After about five hours of walking through forest terrain, Dianne finally came to "Zebras: What a Wonder!" Aaron felt ready to grab Dianne, crumple her like an old grocery list, and shove her in a trash can, or perhaps a hollowed log, in the absence of trash cans in the middle of the woods.

But finally, silence—for about ten seconds anyhow. Dianne soon delighted in using her magic to change his hair into different colors—blue, purple, bluish-purple, bleach-blonde, hot pink. *Which isn't so bad,* he thought, *so long as I can't see it myself, and so long as I don't have to hear her incessant chattering. Nothing could be worse than that...*

But then he discovered something *could* be worse—her incessant giggling. Every time she would change his hair a new color, she would giggle in delight and soon proceeded to transform his entire wardrobe as well.

She was finally pleased when he wore an orange-and-black-striped tunic, red-and-white polka-dotted shirt, pink and yellow hair, and one red eye and one black eye, which looked quite disturbing as one eye "looked possessed" and the other as though nothing but a hole gaped there, so she decided to give him back his, "old, boring, ordinary brown eyes."

After a couple more hours of "fun," Dianne finally grew tired, returned Aaron to his original appearance, and slipped into his pocket, falling into a deep slumber.

He felt quite relieved that she changed him back to normal before falling asleep because after traveling the same direction for about another hour or so— Dianne had mumbled, "Just keep going west," before snoring loudly—he stepped from the trees to behold the garden they sought.

CHAPTER 13

The garden was surrounded by a great wall over-laden with ivy. Set in the wall was a tall, narrow, pearl-white tower. The tower held a single door below and a single window above. As Aaron approached, someone drew back from the window. He had been seen. He paused, waiting and wondering.

The door swung open, and a flood of the purest, whitest light poured out, and through the enlightened doorway stepped a fair maid whose beauty surpassed that of any who lived or would ever live in all of Zephyr's islands.

A rosy glow sparkled on her golden curls which framed her face and brushed her shoulders. Her dress shimmered, a white iridescent silk, the rainbow colors altering in the light. She wore a crystal pendant and earrings, through which the light shone like prisms, dispersing all around her in every color of the spectrum. Her eyes were like prisms too, glinting with first violet, then blue, then green. Those same eyes also held a very strong gaze. At present, they were calm, peaceful, and welcoming, but Aaron did not think he should like to know how they looked when she grew angry. In some strange sense, she reminded him of a much more elegant Mrs. Daniels.

"Welcome," she called in a soft, yet strong, clear voice. "Welcome to the Garden of Mirism. I am Amanda Danielle, the keeper thereof. Your name is well known here, Aaron, Hero of 1,000 years. Do not be afraid. We are safe from all who might wish to hear of our plans once we enter the garden. Enter the light."

As he stepped into the tower, the light almost blinded him, but Amanda Danielle gently took his hand and led him up the tower steps. He guessed that she must have lived here a very long time to be able to look upon such pure, bright light.

Finally, they stopped and she commanded him to open his eyes. Brightness yet enshrouded them, but the light had lessened enough so that he could comfortably look around. Upon spotting a window, he determined they must stand at the top of the tower.

Amanda turned and faced him, beaming a radiant, diamond-glow smile. "You pass the test. Only those who try to serve Amiel and the cause of right truly can pass through the White Light. Those with a black heart, such as Rorrim, would not even be able to look upon the tower.

"But come. Now is not the time for talk, for there is much to be done."

His eyes roamed to a door opposite the window.

As she opened the door and walked through, Aaron followed.

They crossed a bridge that stretched to another tower, walking over the garden. Aaron could see many bright, blossoming flowers, luscious trees, and sparkling streams and falls below. Also, he noted a thick patch of trees where streams of light shot out at different angles, as if reflected from a great mirror. They crossed over to the other tower, a simple stone structure laden with ivy, like the wall surrounding the garden.

Walking through the door, they wound down the stairs. Then they passed through another door and found themselves inside the garden.

Rich life surrounded them—flowers of every shade, including megflowers holding glistening gems and soft green grass scrolling like velvet beneath their feet. Amanda Danielle tread barefoot, her gentle footfall creating no noise as they walked, making his own, restrained footsteps sound like awkward thunder in his ears.

Thebaziles and butterflies, deer and rabbits all flitted about, and Aaron thought he even caught a glimpse of a phoenix.

The air smelled pure and the water flowed clear and crystal like glass, a pleasantly cool breeze blew at perfectly timed intervals, or so it seemed, for he was not too hot nor too cold.

Yet they passed the beauty of the gardens and came to the place Aaron viewed from the bridge, where the trees thickly knit together, and here Amanda paused, he beside her.

"Now you shall see why this place has been called the 'Garden of Endless Lights.'"

As soon as they stepped through the door, Amanda closed and locked it behind them, and Aaron found himself staring in wonder.

Everywhere, scattered all through the trees, hovered rings of light like the portal Liv had showed him.

They all shone with a brilliant, white light, yet each held within it a picture of someplace or someone. As they walked along in slow, quiet reverence, Amanda explained, "There are many places that contain portals of time and space, but this garden contains more than any in the world."

As they weaved in and out of portals, Aaron spotted many different events within—a fisherman fishing, two knights jousting, a man in a space suit walking on the moon, something that looked like a battle scene from World War II, and a man giving a speech Aaron thought looked very much like Abraham Lincoln...

But they slipped past all these, stopping instead before an ivory pedestal standing between two trees. Beneath each of these two trees stood a portal, and upon the pedestal lay a simple wooden box glowing with a faded, golden light.

As Amanda stood on one side of the pedestal, Aaron stood on the other, peering down curiously at the box. It appeared plain, except for words ornately carved on top.

As Aaron read them in his head, Amanda read them aloud, "*Emit Nepo, Emit Levart, Emit Eclos.*" Immediately, the lid of the box shot open, something glowing brightly from within.

Aaron's attention drew to the object as Amanda rested it in her palm. It was a green, semi-transparent, smooth, sparkling stone, and perfectly triangular in shape. It hung upon a golden chain.

"This is the ancient treasure of the Scintillate and Mira people—the Emit Enots, the stone of time. It is very rare, albeit, there are two others like it.

"Aaron..." She stared right into his eyes with her powerful gaze. "Do you know why Rorrim tried to kill you?"

Aaron shook his head.

"It is because he knew that someday you would hold one of these Destiny stones in your hands. This stone I pass to you—" As Amanda Danielle set it in his hands, it felt very light in weight yet strangely made his whole body feel heavy. "—contains the power to unlock all portals of time and space, including that which will take you to your own time.

"You must guard it carefully though. This stone holds the key you need to undo Rorrim's evil plot, yet should he obtain all three stones himself, he could use them against you.

"You must return now to your time and protect the bearers of the other stones. Rorrim will be searching for them as well."

"Who are the others?"

Amanda did not answer, or at least not in words. But her gaze shifted, and Aaron's gaze followed hers.

Inside one of the portals, he caught a glimpse of a face he knew quite well. The vision flickered, but the snatches he saw were enough.

"Chasmira," he breathed.

"You know her?" Amanda's voice did not contain any tone of surprise, as if the great fairy *expected* him to know Chasmira.

As Aaron started towards the portal, Amanda Danielle's gaze lingered upon him with careful watchfulness. But something stopped him, a voice calling his name, a voice *shrieking* his name, and then the sound of horse's hooves and neighing.

He whirled. On the opposite side of the pedestal, beneath the other tree, glittered the other portal. The picture in this one was clearer and did not fade. It showed Liv running with fright-filled eyes, and as she glanced over her shoulder, the scene scrolled to the side to reveal a black-suited archer pursuing her on his ebony steed and shooting black arrows at her.

A sick feeling filled Aaron as he saw himself faced with an immediate, serious decision. Perhaps he could rescue Liv and hurry with her to the thousand-year portal where he would reach Chasmira before a darker force did.

He called to Amanda Danielle over his shoulder, "Good-bye! Thanks for everything!" Then, he took a great leap into the portal.

CHAPTER 14

Liv looked up in surprise to see Aaron running beside her.

"Aaron," she cried, "Rorrim knows who you are. He tried to get me to tell him where you were, but I escaped. Quick! The portal approaches!"

The closed portal loomed before them in the not so far distance; for some reason, the trees seemed to have stood aside, revealing it clearly. He shouted instinctively, "Emit Nepo!"

The door swung open and light gushed forth. Aaron broke into a sprint and shouted, "Come on! We're almost there!"

Suddenly, a cry pierced the air behind Aaron, and he turned. Liv slouched to the ground, clutching her bleeding leg. He started towards her, but she held up her free hand, pleading, "No! Go on without me."

"But—" he protested, eyes gleaming with torture as his desire to obey restrained him from helping her.

"I'll be fine, but the barrier—go before he reaches us!"

Aaron gazed at the approaching black archer and ducked as one of the raven arrows streaked past.

"*Go!*" cried Liv.

Finally, reluctantly, Aaron broke from that urgent gaze, sprinting towards the portal.

CHAPTER 15

Aaron surged through the portal, finally reemerging in his own time.

"Chasmira, Nathan, everyone, I'm back—"

He stopped abruptly, realizing he stood in an empty wood, in a huge, muddy clearing where the mansion once stood. Only the school's gardens remained. Had he been gone *that* long? Was he too late to save everyone already?

Then, feeling a shadow cloaking his body, he looked up and took in his breath. The entire campus floated high above him. He was in over his head.

Where to begin this time? Who was he fooling by accepting this Hero's quest?

* * *

When Chasmira awoke, she thought perhaps she was still outside, for darkness enshrouded her. She felt the hard, cold surface stretching beneath her.

Sitting up, it took her eyes a few moments to adjust to the darkness. But then, as they focused, she found herself in a dungeon cell. One wall was completely constructed of iron bars, allowing her to see clearly that her cell was only one of about ten or so tracing the perimeter of a shadowy, circular room.

Nothing else was in the room until a prick of light appeared in the center. It grew and opened wide, and through it stepped a man dressed in black. He held a struggling girl close to him.

Chasmira could not see his face beyond his black hood, but the girl was very pretty. Her dark waves of hair fell long over her shoulder, her wide eyes shone a lovely midnight blue, and she dressed in a red and white silk gown much resembling Chasmira's costume.

Quickly laying back down, Chasmira pretended to be asleep as the light closed behind the man and girl. He threw the girl in the cell next to Chasmira's, hissing, "Now, you'll stay in there and cause me no more trouble. I have some further business to attend to..."

As Chasmira cracked one eye open, she saw him set a sword and shield on the ground. They were clear and sparkling as if made of glass.

"I doubt your friend will get far without these..."

95

He exited the door on the far side of the room, his footsteps receding as he wound up the stairs.

"Drat," Chasmira heard the girl say. "*Now* how will I get help to Aaron...?"

At Aaron's name, Chasmira shot up. "You know Aaron?"

The girl gasped. "Who's there?"

"My name's Chasmira. I'm in the cell next to yours."

"Do you know Aaron too?"

"Yes. We're friends, but how do you—?"

"I'm Liv, and I'll explain later. First, we must get these weapons to Aaron, but how—?

"Taylor!"

"At your service!" Taylor said brightly.

"Who?" asked Chasmira.

"It's Taylor, my guardian fairy.

"I didn't know you followed me here."

"A guardian fairy never deserts her master or mistress."

"Well, I'm certainly glad to see you. The girl in the next cell is Chasmira. She's friends with Aaron. The friend he told us of, I believe—"

"Ooo, Aaron, the cute one—"

"*And*, we need some way to warn him—the Dark Master has some sort of barrier surrounding the school, and a dragon. We need someone to warn Aaron and get that sword and shield to him."

"Hmm...I could deliver the message, but the items are far too heavy..."

They all fell silent, disappearing into deep thought again.

Then, Chasmira exclaimed, "I know! Taylor, do you think you could find a girl named Rachel? She's somewhere inside the school, uhh, red ponytail, glasses, very short, loves to read—"

"I'm on it!" Taylor shouted, and Chasmira caught a glimpse of her as she slipped out Liv's window.

CHAPTER 16

While Aaron had attended his adventure, all the students had been sent to their dorms by the mysterious man in black, who appeared along with a horde of black-clad servants who called him the "Dark Master." All the teachers were locked in Mr. Root's office, sealed in by powerful magic.

Everyone prayed or tried to figure out what was going on, except certain people like Krystal who was concerned with the nail she'd broken when the girl dressed as a popsicle bumped into her and she fell.

Many theories floated about, such as the school was abducted by aliens, or mutant insects, or that Josh was really the man in black and pulled a prank, but then all concluded that such a prank was too magnificent for Josh to imagine. In fact, he was still in his cheese costume, having trouble even getting through doorways. Many were reminded of the stories they had read about the wicked clan of fairies known as Mass which had attacked the school before, but then they reminded themselves that all the Mass items were destroyed long ago.

So in the end, no one knew anything more than when they started—that a maniac in black had taken over the school and put it in the air for unknown reasons.

Well, Rachel *did* know something else—she was bored and annoyed.

Tiffany could at least do homework. Krystal had filed the same nail for the last half hour, mumbling irritably about "people who dress as popsicles." Hailey stared out the window, lost in her own world, humming and smiling in her usual fashion.

Rachel *didn't even feel like reading*. She wanted to do something constructive—discover where Chasmira had vanished to, or, for Jiminy cricket's sake, find out where Aaron had disappeared to. She knew zip of their situation, and it drove her mad. The itchy tape on her glasses was still driving her crazy too.

Hailey was humming the song from her favorite Wal-mart commercial for the third time, and Rachel was about to yell, "Snapperdoodle!" in frustration, when something caught Rachel's eye. The doorknob was moving, wiggling as if someone tried to break in.

The others noticed it too and glanced nervously at each other. Rachel stood back and drew her sword. Of course, it was only plastic, but it could still come in handy for jabbing someone in the eye should the need arise.

Suddenly, the door opened a crack and then closed, but no one appeared to have entered the room. Was it a ghost? None of them believed in ghosts, but the day had proved so weird already...

But then a bright light flew up from the floor—whatever it was must've entered from below—and then Taylor flew so that she hovered level with their faces. "I'm looking for Rachel Miner. Which of you—?"

"That's me," said Rachel quickly.

Taylor turned to Rachel and bowed. "I am Taylor, servant of Liv, princess of destiny past, and Chasmira, princess of destiny future. I was sent to fetch you. The princesses are in need of your help."

Thousands of questions swam in Rachel's head, but she asked what she had wondered for so long now, what seemed most important, "Is Chasmira all right?"

"She is held prisoner in the clutches of the black-cloaked gentleman, but she is unharmed, yes."

"Where is she?"

"A secret dungeon beneath the school."

"Can you show me how to get there?"

"I'm not sure. I've been flying in and out of windows, which I'm afraid you can't do since they're all barred."

Rachel's heart sank, but in the next moment, it rose. She'd once read of a secret passage in the school leading to underground, secret rooms, but it was located in the entrance hall which was sure to be heavily guarded.

"Taylor, how hard would it be to sneak down to the entrance hall?"

"Hmm...several black-caped men have been patrolling the halls, yet...I believe it could be done..."

"Let's get to it then."

As Rachel started towards the door, Krystal frowned. "Wait—you can't just *leave*. What if—if *he* comes? What are we going to tell him when he finds you've escaped?"

Rachel sighed impatiently. "Just...lock the bathroom door and say I'm in there. Yeash, it's not that difficult..."

Sneaking past the guards turned out to be even less difficult. Most of them had escaped to the kitchen for a snack break, according to Taylor. They were supposed to take turns leaving their posts, but it seemed they grew hungry all at once. As she smiled slyly, Rachel wondered if their sudden hunger had anything to do with her magic.

Finding the secret passage in the hall was a synch as well, thanks to Rachel's extensive reading and memory. All they had to do was find the trap door made to look like one of the tiles in the floor, remove it, slip under, then gently replace the tile, though not quite all the way so they could get back out. The tile rested under a table with a long tablecloth, so no one was bound to see. The scheme was almost too easy to be believable.

As Chasmira saw Rachel racing down the spiral steps and through the doorway, she looked up with a surprised gasp.

"Rachel!"

Rachel raced to Chasmira's cell, pressing her face against the bars.

"Boy, what a dump! We need to get you outta here."

"Actually," said Liv. "It's really quite clean for a prison."

Rachel jumped and looked over at Liv. "Who's that?"

"I am Liv, princess of destiny past." She nodded her head, and Rachel did the same.

"Looks like I'm rescuing *both* of you then."

"No." Chasmira shook her head. "There's no time for that. Only Aaron can save the school, and he's on his way now. You have to take that shield and sword to him."

Rachel turned and saw the sword and shield. How did she miss them before?

She hefted the crystal blade. It felt so light-weight, but its sharp edges gleamed, warning it was not a weapon to be underestimated.

Suddenly, footsteps echoed on the stairs.

"It's him!" hissed Chasmira in a panicked whisper.

Chasmira laid down, feigning sleep once more.

But as she heard the Dark Master enter the room yet heard no other noise, she peeked her eye open. Rachel was nowhere in sight, and the shield lay on the ground as before, but where was the sword? And where was Rachel?

Presently, one of the black-caped men appeared and bowed to the Dark Master.

"Master," he panted, obviously in quite a rush, "one of the prisoners, Rachel Miner, is missing..."

"What? Blasted fools, can't keep your eyes on a few school girls—" But in the midst of his ranting, the Dark Master stopped. As he stepped towards the lonely shield, Chasmira felt her heart sink.

Chasmira heard a gasp and looked up. Rachel and Taylor hovered in the air, as close to the ceiling as possible; Taylor had evidently turned Rachel's shoes into hoverboots.

Chasmira's eyes widened, and then she quickly realized what she was doing and turned her gaze back to the Dark Master. But he glared menacingly at her, and then he scrolled his eyes upward.

He drew a black sword and mumbled something beneath his breath. Dark shadows clustered around the sword's tip, and as he swung the blade, a black mass surged towards Rachel.

"Use the Crystal!" shouted Taylor, and Rachel raised the crystal sword just in time to reflect the attack back at him.

The Dark Master leapt aside to avoid the counter-attack, and as the black mass struck the floor, a great explosion boomed, dust and smoke filling the room.

This offered Rachel plenty of time to snatch up the shield and flee the room, zooming swiftly upon air. She shuddered, picking up speed as the dark lord shouted, "Don't just stand there coughing like an idiot! After her!"

Rachel swept up the stairs, out of the dungeons, and up to the second floor, subconsciously making her way to Nathan's dorm.

"Taylor, can you open this door?"

"What?"

"Just do it!" Rachel cried, shoving Taylor in the keyhole.

Rachel glanced down the hallways, expecting to see one of the black men appear, but none did. Finally, the door swung open and Rachel flew in, slamming it shut and locking it behind them.

She found Josh, Nathan and Sam—Josh was still dressed as giant cheese—sitting on one of the beds playing "Go Fish."

"Yeah!" Josh exclaimed. "She's come to rescue us!"

"Rachel?" Nathan sat up, studying Rachel with a curious frown. "What—?"

"Aaron's in trouble, and we need to get this sword and shield to him, and some weirdo's chasing me, and I don't really want to go alone—"

"I'm ready." Nathan hopped up.

Someone banged on the door.

"Open up! Rorrim's command!"

Rachel's eyes widened.

"*It's him.*"

Nathan jerked his head to the side. "The window."

"But—"

"Sam used a charm to remove the bars."

As Nathan swung the window open, Josh said, "Uhh, could you get this zipper thing unstuck first? This cheese outfit's getting really hot—"

"No time, Josh." Rachel hopped out the window after Nathan.

They could hear Josh crying, "Aww, man!" as they flew towards the dark, semi-transparent barrier surrounding the floating school grounds.

"How do we get through *that?*" Nathan asked.

"The sword," explained Rachel quickly.

But something zoomed down from the sky, knocking the sword from her hand, and it plunged to the earth far below.

"What the—?" began Nathan, but Rachel shouted, "Move!" and yanked him out of harm's way as two black arrows shot past. Looking up, they saw two black archers hovering only feet away and setting more arrows to their strings.

"There's no use standing—er, flying—no, that's not it, umm...hovering? Well, whatever, let's get the sword and move!" Rachel darted towards the ground, Nathan following her.

They quickly found the sword, and Rachel sheathed it, but they were faced with another problem. Half a dozen black archers had assembled and closed in from above.

"We'll have to fight," decided Rachel, as she and Nathan drew swords.

"But all we have are these cheesy plastic things."

"No problem!" Taylor zipped around each of their swords, sprinkling fairy dust on each. The swords glowed, lengthened, and transformed into pure sapphire blades. "Now," quipped Taylor, "what you must know about sapphire blades is that they are not only very durable but also hold the power and accuracy to bounce arrows right back at whoever shoots them, or to hit any object back to wherever the object came from, and were thus sometimes called baseball blades—"

"All right!" cried Nathan as a rain of black arrows showered upon them. They blocked the spiraling arrows with their swords, volleying them right back at the archers who hurried to dodge their own weapons.

"Come on." Rachel sped with Nathan towards the barrier.

"How will we get out?"

Rachel drew the crystal blade and sheathed her sapphire blade. "I need you to fend them off for me, and I'll make a hole in the barrier."

As they neared the barrier, two dozen black archers appeared and catapulted towards them, bows and arrows ready to shoot.

"Rachel," Nathan panicked, "hurry—we're going to crash into the barrier—"

"No, we're not..."

Just before they *did* crash into it, Rachel swung the sword, slitting a large opening in the barrier and they passed through, just as another shower of arrows rained towards them.

"Phew," breathed Nathan as they retreated into the woods. "That was close."

Something rumbled loudly, and Rachel raised her brow. "Nathan..."

"No, that was *not* my stomach—"

It echoed again. Slowly and with definite reluctance, they turned to stare into the eyes of a great dragon. Its scales were a deep black, and a ridge of blue scales bristled along its backbone. The dragon was long and snaky with no arms or legs but small, bat-like wings and flashed lethal fangs.

As its onyx eyes burned with rage, Rachel gaped fearfully and Nathan pulled her out of the way as the dragon's fangs struck.

"What the heck is that?" Nathan cried.

"That must be the monster Rorrim said can only be destroyed with the crystal blade."

"But there's only *one* crystal blade."

"Exactly. I'll fight, and you just keep safe."

She handed him the shield and drew the sword, jumping from the bushes to face the dragon.

"Rachel—!"

"Don't worry!" she called over her shoulder. "It'll be just like the battles on all the Loz games—!"

Nathan could only watch, peering from beneath the shield as Rachel dodged the dragon's teeth and claws and tried vainly to land in some of her own blows. She seemed to be waste all her energy merely dodging. Finally, Nathan rushed at the dragon, shouting. If his sword would do no damage, perhaps he could at least distract the beast.

This seemed to prove fruitful, for as the dragon turned his attention towards Nathan, Rachel stabbed the monster's tail. When she jabbed him a few more times though, he shrieked madly, his eyes flashing with a violent promise that these children would *not* get the best of him.

Wrapping his tail around Nathan, he flung him against a tree. Nathan lay motionless, stunned. As Rachel rushed to help him, Taylor darted around the dragon's head, but this only made him release an agitated roar and flick her aside with his tail.

As Rachel knelt over Nathan, he began to wake, groaning.

A shadow passed over them, and she turned to see the dragon pulling his head back, ready to lunge. She hefted her sword high, but instead of biting her, he whipped his tail around, knocking the sword from her hands, quickly coiling his tail around her and flying high into the sky.

Higher they rose, above the clouds, even above the hovering school, and Rachel's heart sank as she realized what the dragon prepared to do. He paused for one, dreadful moment, and then released his grasp on her.

As she plunged towards the earth, she let fly a horrific scream. But as she plummeted towards the trees, someone shot from them, catching her in his arms. Nathan...?

No, it was Aaron, and she was never more glad to see him in all her life. She would later say how she would've preferred that Nathan save her, but when you're plummeting towards the ground after being dropped by a dragon from hundreds of feet in the sky, you really can't be picky, can you?

Aaron safely set her on the ground, found the sword, grabbed it, and zoomed back up to face the dragon.

"When'd Aaron get here?" Rachel asked Nathan.

"Just now. I gave him my boots. Won't do me any good with my broken leg."

"It's broke—? *Jiminy cricket, Aaron?*" Rachel stared into the sky.

"What's going on?" Nathan tried to swerve his body so he could also look up but groaned at the painful movement.

Aaron hovered in mid-air as the dragon lunged towards him, but at the last moment, he lifted the shield, and the dragon banged his head on it and fell back with a loud screech.

While the dragon shook his head, partially stunned, Aaron flew in and stabbed the creature's soft belly.

The monster lurched for him again, but instead of darting left or right, Aaron flew up so that the dragon chomped his own tail instead.

"Wow," breathed Nathan as Rachel explained it all, though it was a wonder how he understood her fast, hyper explanations, "no joke, so *that's* why he's on the Hover-ball team..."

Aaron soared swiftly up, and Dianne shouted, "Now, right for his heart!" She threw her fairy dust upon the sword to guide its aim, and Aaron jabbed the dragon straight through his chest.

Aaron flew back as the creature writhed, screaming in pain, and then disintegrated like dust. The barrier encompassing the school shattered like glass, the pieces dissolving into dust before dissipating into nothing.

Aaron soared with Dianne back to where Rachel helped Nathan sit up against a tree.

"Aaron, that was *awesome!*" she exclaimed.

"Thanks." He then turned to Nathan who winced. "You gonna be okay?"

"Sure, he is," quipped Dianne as she and Taylor, whom Dianne revived, flew up to him.

"We'll have him as good as new in no time," added Taylor.

The two circled his leg.

"Hey, thanks." All pain faded from his face, and he stood up.

"No problem," smiled Taylor as Dianne flew up to him and asked, "And who is this?"

"This is Nathan," said Aaron, "and here's Rachel."

"Ooo, I like him." Dianne fluttered very close to Nathan's face, which turned very red.

"Well," said Aaron loudly, shooing Dianne away from Nathan, "that was certainly exciting."

"Oh, yes, I love barrier breaking," chirped Dianne, eyes gleaming enthusiastically. "It's just like in 'To the Ends of the Earth,' from 'The Legends of Surprisers.'"

Rachel smirked. "Oh, I like her."

"*Okay*," said Aaron even more forcefully, wanting very quickly to stray from the subject of books before Rachel and Dianne delved into a detailed conversation. "Now that we've all been introduced, let's stop and rest a while and figure out what to do next."

Everyone agreed with this. Fighting a dragon had proved quite taxing work.

CHAPTER 17

They found the place where the school's garden pond still remained and refreshed themselves by taking a long, cool drink. Rachel and Aaron removed their boots, dangling their feet in the pond.

As the three rested, Dianne and Taylor soon discovered the thrill of being able to change Rachel's, Aaron's, and Nathan's hair color all at once. Rachel was completely content when their hair changed blue, claiming that it made her really look like Adelyn from "Loz: Final Quest," especially as she still wore her costume. On top of that, Dianne knew a spell to fix her glasses so that they no longer drove her insane.

"We should make their hair purple—wouldn't that look dashing on Nathan?" suggested Dianne.

"But green is totally Aaron's color," argued Taylor.

Dianne did not look happy. It was obvious Taylor would not let her have her own way easily. For the next few moments, Aaron's, Rachel's, and Nathan's hair flashed from green to purple, back and forth. All the while, Taylor's and Dianne's expressions grew more annoyed and stubbornly determined, and more and more sparks flew from them.

Suddenly, the fairies gasped as Aaron, Rachel, and Nathan disappeared.

"Did we—did we invisibilize them?" Taylor cried, panicking.

"Uhh—" stammered Dianne.

"Oh, this is *not* even funny—"

"Coolio!"

"I always wondered what it was like to be two inches tall—this is *awesome*!"

At this, Dianne and Taylor looked down, then at each other guiltily. They had accidentally used a shrinking spell!

As the two fairies spiraled down to join their now-tiny companions, Aaron stomped towards Dianne, fuming. "Okay, what did you do, and how do we get out of this mess?"

"Umm..." Dianne glanced nervously at Taylor who only replied, "Don't look at *me*—*I* don't remember the counter spell."

"Aww, great..."

"I *do* remember reading about it in 'Spells of Shrinkage,' though," mused Dianne.

"Oh, of course you'd remember what *book* it's in—"

"Chillax, Aaron," said Rachel. "We'll just find the book in the school library and fix this."

"And how do you expect to get there?"

Rachel opened her mouth to answer him but then noticed the normal-sized hoverboots lying next to the pond and cried, "Aww, snap!"

"Can you just shrink the shoes too?" Nathan asked Taylor.

Taylor blushed. "Well...we don't actually *know* the shrinking spell—we just run across it by accident every now and then. Like, once we shrunk this lady's feet and she couldn't walk for a month—"

"That's enough encouragement," Aaron decided. "Let's get going."

"How?" asked Rachel.

"Well..." Aaron cast a playful grin at Dianne. "They got us into this mess, so they can have the honor of carrying us."

Of course, that was their only option, but it didn't work very well. Dianne carried Aaron, and Taylor carried Rachel but held her in such a way that she kept tickling her; Rachel laughed so hard that Taylor nearly dropped her several times.

When they finally reached the school, one of the windows thankfully happened to be cracked open. Taylor and Dianne quickly deposited their burdens on the floor, worn out from carrying them, since Nathan had proved no help. He had only flitted around, gloating that *he* could fly and *they* couldn't.

When everyone stood inside, they started towards the library.

Nathan moaned. "It'll take forever to get there on these tiny legs..."

Jarrett suddenly rounded the corner. He was sleepwalking.

Aaron, Nathan, Rachel, Dianne and Taylor all looked at each other with expressions that told they were all thinking the same thing.

They waited until Jarrett walked past them and then leapt on his leg and scurried up to his shoulders. After seating themselves, Aaron leaned over and whispered in Jarrett's ear, "Jarrett...there's a big pizza waiting for you in the library."

"Li...bary..." Jarrett mumbled.

"Yep. Now go to the right..."

They all continued to give Jarrett directions…,

"Left."

"No, that's right."

"*Big* pizza, don't forget..."

"Whoa, don't fall down the stairs—"

"Oops, turn around—that's the math room, not the library..."

This procedure worked quite well until Nathan accidentally turned Jarrett into a wall. He walked right into it, bumping his nose, then stood with his head against the wall, snoring loudly. For all their efforts, they couldn't get him to budge again.

"Good going, Nathan," Rachel mumbled.

"Ooo, now what do we do?" cried Dianne in frustration.

But someone else approached. It was Sam, treading noiselessly down the hallway.

"Nathan," said Aaron. "Go get Sam."

Nathan nodded and flew up to Sam's ear, whispering, "Sam. Hey, Sam."

Sam froze in his tracks, his gaze flitting about the room.

"Who's there?"

"Sam, over here."

Sam turned full-circle as Nathan perched on his shoulder.

"Boy, I've been sitting in that room with Josh too long. Now I'm hearing his voice in my head..."

"Sam, you nut! It's *me*, Nathan!"

"Nathan? Where *are* you?"

As Nathan flew up in Sam's face, he squealed in surprise, stumbling backwards. Rachel, Taylor, Dianne, and Aaron burst out laughing, Aaron snickering, "Well, the one thing that *hasn't* changed in this place is *he* still squeals like a girl..."

When Sam regained his balance, he focused upon Nathan, squinting very hard, as if to be sure of what he really saw.

"Nathan? Is that really you? How in the—?"

"Don't even ask. Look, we need someone to carry us to the library, but Jarrett's shut down over there. Can you give us a lift?"

"Who's 'us?'"

"Me, Aaron, Rachel, and two fairies named Taylor and Dianne."

"You're *all* shrunk? And who are—?"

"Like I said, don't even ask. I'll explain later."

When Aaron and Nathan settled themselves on one of Sam's shoulders, the girls perching on the other, Dianne complaining that his shoulder was very bony and uncomfortable, Sam started towards the library.

"So, how'd you get out?" Aaron asked Sam.

"Well," whispered Sam, "Josh wanted me to go find some scissors or something to get him out of his cheese costume, so we picked the lock to our door. I planned to make a detour to the kitchen too—we're starving. Anyhow, I've only had to get past two guards so far, so I figured I may as well try the kitchen. What's so important about the library, anyhow?"

"Well," said Aaron. "Dianne and Taylor *conveniently* forgot the reverse spell for shrinking, but *of course* Dianne remembers what book it's in—" Dianne squinted at him and stuck out her tongue. "—and we can't save Chasmira like this either."

"Chasmira?" Sam's face flashed sudden concern. "Is she all right?"

"Yeah, sure, she'll be fine," said Aaron casually, though his eyes flickered with uncertainty.

Finally, they reached the library, delving into the maze of book-and-dust-packed shelves.

"Which book is it?" asked Sam.

"'Spells of Shrinkage,'" replied Rachel. "I've seen it in the magic section."

They made their way to the aisle titled "Spells," but as Sam browsed through the books, he groaned.

"What now?" hissed Aaron.

"Josh and Caleb played one of their classic jokes again—these are all science books, mostly on dissection..."

"Me, Taylor, and Nathan will fly around and look for the magic books," suggested Dianne.

"Okay," agreed Sam, as the three fairies flew off. "We'll check the Science area."

After several minutes, Nathan flew back to report that the magic books were located in the math section.

"There's a section for *math* books?" asked Aaron as Sam carried him and Rachel over. "Who would go *there?* They must've *really* wanted to hide those spell books..."

It was too dim to see the words on the pages of the books—the only light came from several pale lamps hanging on the walls—but Dianne and Taylor each produced a small globe of light, hovering them over the book as Sam leafed through the pages.

"Coolio," Rachel breathed, staring over his shoulder. "It's totally written in Ancient Lozolian...."

Aaron rolled his eyes. "Oh, you *would...*"

Suddenly, Dianne squealed, "There it is!" and Taylor cried, "Read it! Read it!"

Sam read it, though with a perplexed look on his face, "Two swishes, one flick, and a jab?"

"Yep, that's it." Dianne nodded. "I always confuse it with the color purple, which has only one swish..."

"So let's do it," said Aaron.

"Uhh, would you mind getting off my shoulders first?" Sam asked.

"Wait." Rachel's brow furrowed thoughtfully. "Wouldn't it be easier to sneak down as little people to the entrance hall and then change?"

Aaron and Nathan pondered a moment before Nathan replied, "The lady's right. It's a good plan."

"Sam, do you think you can take us to the entrance hall?" Aaron asked.

"Sure thing."

CHAPTER 18

Chasmira looked up as soft footsteps padded towards her, hoping they didn't signal Rorrim's return.

But then Aaron, Rachel, and Nathan strode through the door, all rushing to Chasmira's cell.

"You came," gasped Chasmira. "You're finally here."

"Did you think we wouldn't come?" Aaron asked.

"I didn't mean that." Chasmira turned her gaze downward. "What I meant was, well, I don't deserve it. The way I yelled at you, Aaron, Nathan—"

"You had a right to be angry."

"Perhaps I did. But I had no right to treat you like that. *I* wasn't a good friend either, and I'm sorry."

"Hey." Aaron flashed his crooked smile, "It's all right. Apology accepted."

"Apology accepted," Nathan agreed, nodding.

Chasmira smiled, and Aaron said, "Now, let's see about getting you and Liv out of here..."

Aaron felt a cold shadow pass over him. As Chasmira's eyes widened in fear, he, Rachel, and Nathan turned to behold the black-cloaked, black-hooded Dark Master towering over him.

"Well, well, Mr. Ruiz, we meet at last. I know many things about you, so I suppose you deserve to know everything about *us*. As one of the keepers of the Destiny Stones, I suppose that makes you my equal in some sense...

"But first, we have not been *properly* introduced, have we? No..."

The man drew back his hood.

"I am Rorrim, the Dark Master who shall soon take over the Lozolian Realm, starting with your petty school.

"Behold, my true self."

Rorrim's form instantly changed, and instead of a hideous figure, they saw a man that was actually quite handsome. He was pure Prismatic, his hair shimmering with all the colors of the rainbow. His iridescent eyes pierced them with a cruel coldness, and Aaron suppressed a shiver.

"Who *are* you exactly?" Chasmira asked. "How have you been in the school the whole time and no one ever noticed?"

"A clever thought, girl," Rorrim admitted, nodding in her direction. "The answer there lies in the fact that, for the most part, I haven't been in the school at all. Rather, a student of this school, one who has long served me, the one who tried to aid me by trying to kill you on several occasions—it is he who did most of the work at the beginning. Though, by his sloppiness I yet wonder if his heart was properly in it. At any rate, his mother rather furious; she is dealing with him now for his poor performance."

"But why here?" Aaron asked. "Why capture a school? And why capture Chasmira and Liv? Why not just kill them and take the stones?"

"A fair question," Rorrim continued coolly. "You see, many before me have tried to take over the Lozolian Realm starting with Zephyr's Islands. But why rule in only the present when you can rule in the past and future as well?

"When I first discovered the power my Destiny Stone held—" He revealed his own, triangular, shining stone, a larger version of the one Amanda Danielle had given Aaron. "—I began a search to learn more. I discovered that there were two others, one of which had been broken in pieces. Separately, they could each only *open* portals of time and space. But combined, they possessed the power to *close and seal* portals forever. Why, I could send *all* the great leaders—Cleocatriss, Lynn, Chryselda Sofia, Zorya, even Zephyr herself—into some dark abyss for all eternity, leaving me free to take over any and every kingdom from every time period in Loz's history.

"But I knew I must start with the ones who held the other stones, the ones who knew their power, who could wield them, who could become my undoing, who could use the stones to banish me back to the place from which I came.

"So, I began the search for the Stones after I figured *you* out, Aaron. I wished to capture the school and seal it with the dark dragon's barrier immediately, but I wanted to make sure both the hero and princess of destiny future were trapped inside first so they could not escape. I already knew who *you* were, Aaron, which is why my nephew tried to kill you with the faulty hoverboots and poison candy, attempting to obtain the stone. He actually snuck into the hospital room one night and searched for it, searched your room as well, if his reports were true...

"By then, I surmised you didn't *have* the stone yet. It was yet in Amanda Danielle's garden. Also, I thought you could be a useful tool in bringing the other stone-bearer to me. After all, I didn't know who the princess of destiny future was. I knew about Liv, and though she was very good at slipping from my grasp, I knew my servants would capture her eventually.

"And then, on the night of the ball, my nephew reported Chasmira's green pendant, and I knew. So, I captured the school—but too late. You had already disappeared, and I thought my plans were spoiled. But then I received word you were with Liv, and hope lifted my weary heart again.

"I let you receive your stone—the final stone I needed—from Amanda Danielle, then sent my servant who captured Liv at the last moment. I knew that once you realized Liv and Chasmira were both in my grasp, you would come to save them. If you broke the barrier and defeated the dragon, fine. If it killed you, I could still get the stone as easily as the princesses' stones.

"But now, I am quite honored to be able to meet the Hero of 1,000 Years— and to bring his life to a short end myself!"

Rorrim threw his cloak over Aaron's face, temporarily blinding him. Upon freeing himself, Rorrim had opened a portal in the midst of the room. It did not shine with the brilliance of those from the gardens but loomed like a great black hole radiating an eerily magnetic power. Aaron forced his gaze to break away, feeling his limbs already grow heavy, succumbing to the portal's pull.

"Now," declared Rorrim, "I will banish you to a land of eternal darkness—"

"Not yet!" Aaron shouted, rushing towards him, sword held high.

Rorrim leapt up and soared out of the way. Nathan and Rachel charged at him with their own swords, but with a sweep of one arm, waves of invisible energy vibrated through the air, knocking them hard against the far wall.

"Aaron, behind you!" cried Liv.

Aaron turned as Rorrim swung a black sword at him and raised the crystal blade. As Rorrim knocked it from his hands, Aaron stumbled backwards towards the dark portal.

As he fell, Rorrim grabbed the stone hanging around his neck. The chain shattered, and Rorrim snatched the stone in his hand. He lifted all three stones triumphantly high, and as Aaron toppled backwards into the dark portal, it snapped shut, Rorrim muttering an incantation with a wicked glee in his eyes.

"Aaron!" shrieked Chasmira.

Rorrim laughed. "You cry in vain, girl! He's been sealed in the past, in the dark, forever, and there he will spend the rest of his miserable days!"

Liv placed a hand on Chasmira's shoulder as she cried bitterly.

"But it is never too late for hope," Liv breathed, glaring at Rorrim.

CHAPTER 19

Aaron shivered as a cold wetness drowned him on all sides. He sat in deep snow, encompassed by an endless canvas of dark and cold. A sharp wind blustered blinding snowflakes all about him, stinging his eyes.

He stood up, shivering. For as far as he could see—which was hardly far at all—a blizzard raged on all sides. He'd been banished to some unknown time and place, a frozen, lifeless wasteland.

Angrily, he beat the snow; the pain of its icy-sharp sting felt good mingled with the pain pressing against his heart.

This is it. I've failed the others. I've failed everything. Chasmira…

"Chasmira…"

He cried out, cursing the storm. Then, the hot tears poured down his cheeks, burning with fire as they froze almost instantly against his skin. Shaking, he fell to his knees and wept.

"Aaron…Aaron…"

At first, it seemed Chasmira's voice called his name. Glancing wildly about, he sought her face, her lovely blue eyes, any sign that she was still close, that only a bad dream now separated them.

When he saw no one, he returned his gaze to the snow, surrendering to another onslaught of silent tears. Perhaps the cold rendered him delirious. Maybe he deserved such a slow, torturous, maddening death.

As the numbing cold began to ripple through every inch of his body, his eyelids began to close slowly, then open again more slowly. He swayed uneasily as a dreamless sleep began to call him, beckoning. Death seemed his truest comfort now. To die and be buried in the snow, his name forgotten forever. His mind began to fade, and hungrily, he accepted the numbness taking hold…

Something burned hotly in his pocket, with a more vehement fire than that of the icy flames licking his flesh as frostbite began its slow dance through his fingers and toes. Jarred back to reality just enough, he reached inside his pocket, pulling out the small object. The green stone he used when they attended the costume ball, his so-called "magic rock."

Yet again, perhaps it *was* magic, for Amanda Danielle's face gazed up at him from the stone's smooth surface. He both saw and heard her call, even more ardently, "Aaron..."

As her eyes met his, he whispered, "Yes, I'm here."

"Aaron," she repeated solemnly. "You of all people—surely you are not giving up hope, giving up on your friends?"

"There's nothing I can do—"

"—giving up on your faith in Amiel?"

Aaron drew silent, a twinge of guilt ringing in his heart.

"Aaron, with Amiel, all things are possible—with Amiel, there's always a way.

"Rorrim is right—with all three stones, he could banish you, Chasmira, Liv, Rachel, the entire school to different times and places, but he would need all three stones."

"But he *has*—"

"Aaron, look at the edge of the stone you hold in your hand."

He turned the stone over until he noticed that one edge was rough, not smooth like the other two.

"The stones Liv and Chasmira held were really fragments that once formed one of the three stones. In the same way, the stone Rorrim obtained just now from you, as well as the one you hold in your hands, are only *fragments* of the same stone. All the stones, whether whole or not, can open portals, but only all three together—and all three must be whole—can seal them. The stone you hold is a fragment of that Rorrim just took from you. It's not too late, Aaron—it's never too late. 'And we know all things work together for good, for them who are called according to His purpose...'"

As her voice and face faded, Aaron felt new determination surging through him. He asked Amiel to forgive him for his momentary lack of faith, imploring much-needed strength as he fulfilled his final mission, then thanked Him for providing the answer.

Lifting the stone high, he shouted, "Emit Nepo, back to Rorrim!"

The stone glowed, the portal opened wide, and Aaron dove into it.

Bursting into the dungeons, he found Rorrim laughing a low, malicious laugh as he rent open another black portal emanating dark power. The gaping hole drew Chasmira, Liv, Nathan, and Rachel towards its horrible grasp. They clawed at the walls and bars of the cells with their bound hands like victims walking towards the edge of a plank, struggling against its magnetic pull, but it was only a matter of time before that pull overcame...

Upon Aaron's arrival, the Destiny Stones began to glow. Rorrim turned, but only in time to see Aaron rushing towards him, sword held high. Aaron's eyes, so often gleaming and sparkling, suddenly became grave, serious, and darkling as he soared towards the man who purposely placed his friends in such peril.

Rorrim's eyes gleamed with a clear wonderment as the young hero surged towards him, sword held high. Wonderment quickly morphed to loathing though, and the moment Aaron reached him, he swung his cape in a wide arc, hoping to ensnare his prey...

Aaron jumped to the side though, weaving between the folds of the cape and landing behind his foe.

"That won't work this time, Rorrim—!"

Rorrim pivoted with a lightning-swift turn, something hit Aaron with the force of a dozen charging soldiers, and he fell hard against the wall behind him. As he hit the hard stone, a pain worse than the fire-ice tendrils of the blizzard shot through the back of his head; his vision blurred, almost blackening, and he sunk to the floor.

His limbs and senses fought to return to the present. The cries of his friends blurred into a fading cacophony of indecipherable noises. He caught a whiff of warm, thick breath and thought Rorrim must stand close, ready to deliver his final strike. As a high shriek pierced through the madness, he knew it was Chasmira. He knew he must get back to her...

Opening his eyes, the dim light of the dungeon blinded him, making his head ache even more ardently. He struggled to stand and face his foe, but his limbs would allow little more than to stagger half-way up the wall before sliding back down again in a defeated slump.

Forcing his eyes to focus past the pain, he gazed up at Rorrim. His cloak was thrown over one shoulder, and he towered over Aaron with a long sword clutched in one of his broad hands, its edges glistening with a silver gleam sharp enough to cut straight through the hearts of many men. Aaron's gaze shifted to Rorrim's other hands, where the Destiny Stones gleamed a brilliant emerald—including the shard Aaron had hoped might save them.

"Before I kill you, boy, there's just one thing I want to know: how? How did this piece of the stones escape my grasp and fall into yours?"

"Ask…Amanda…Danielle," Aaron gasped.

Rorrim's suddenly hardened gaze and Chasmira's terrified crying of his name echoed in his mind as reality faded from him once again and then slipped away entirely.

EPILOGUE

"Sh...he's waking up at last..."

"*This* scene looks familiar, heh."

"Don't be so insensitive, Josh. Jikes, it's not like the poor dude hasn't already almost died, what? *How* many times in the past few weeks..?"

"Aaron..?"

Aaron's ears opened to Chasmira's voice, and upon opened his eyes, hers was the first face he smiled upon.

She looked like she'd been holding her breath a while and released a deep sigh. Worry washed away from her eyes as a smile lit them, softening her face to the familiar one he loved most.

Glancing away from her, he saw Rachel, Nathan, Josh, and Hailey clustered around him. To the side, the nurse changed one of the hospital beds, looking over every now and then to shake her head and *tsk* at them.

"How do you feel, Aaron?"

Aaron returned his gaze to Chasmira; the concern had returned to her face, though not in full force this time.

"Pretty normal, except being tired...

"Umm, so I assume, since I'm here and everyone's here that everything worked out all right, but...how?

Rachel shook her head. "It was weird as all get-out, lemme tell you..."

"Yeah, man," said Josh. "I mean, there you were, all unconscious-like, and we're all getting sucked towards this creepy portal thingy. And then, at the last moment, Rorrim uses the Destiny Stones and banishes *himself* inside."

Aaron stared, almost sitting up in surprise, but a dull pain pulsing in the back of his head made him lay down.

"Before you ask," quipped Hailey, "no one knows why. Although, what you said before blacking out and becoming virtually useless to our cause seemed to disturb him enough that, well, it helped us out anyways. Lucky for you..."

120

"What did *I* say to get him shaken up?" Aaron rubbed his temple, trying to remember, but his mind was a blank canvas.

"It wasn't so much shaken up like he was afraid," Chasmira said. "He looked like you made him suddenly remember a really important appointment he couldn't miss."

"Not even for world-domination," Josh mused.

"It happened when you said Amanda Danielle's name," Chasmira added. "He got that…look in his eyes, that angry but determined sort of look. He mumbled something we couldn't hear, talking to himself. Then, before we knew it, he shouted some magic words, slipped inside the portal, and it snapped shut, gone forever."

Aaron shrugged. "Well, I guess that was convenient."

Rachel snorted. "I'm sure there was more to that creeper than met the eye. He's up to *something*. But at least *we* don't have to deal with him anymore."

Aaron released a deep sigh. Well, that was that. Hero by accident, and the villain was gone. If he'd known it was that easy to get rid of Rorrim, he'd have spoken a random fairy's name a long time ago.

Glancing around again at the sea of faces watching him in anticipation, a small frown crossed his lips and brow. "So…where is Liv, if I may ask?"

"She had to skip back to the past," Chasmira said, "just long enough to gather some of her people. She'll be back soon enough."

"What's she doing?"

"Helping us rebuild the school. They had to put some of the hospital back together to even take *you* here."

Rachel shook her head. "Blasted doorway caved it when that maniac up-rooted the school."

Aaron sighed again. Suddenly realizing how his heart sped, he fought to calm it. It was truly surreal to be knocked unconscious in the midst of a battle against a powerful sorcerer intent on killing you one moment, and wake up what seemed the very next moment and everything was peaceful as it was before.

"Well," he said at last. "I guess that's that. I'm back, *we're* back. Everything is back to normal."

His eyes searched and rested at last upon Chasmira. A brilliant smile lit her face, and pride shone vividly in her gaze. As he forced himself not to look away from her humbling admiration, he knew that, despite how much he wanted to be sure of it, things would never truly be normal ever again, whether for the bad or, for now, the good.

***

The school was once more rooted to the ground, and all had returned to normal—or as normal as things could usually be around Lynn Lectim.

Liv had used the Destiny Stones to summon Mira and Forest-footer elves from the past, and they, along with all the students and staff, managed to repair the damage done to the school. The Mira also brought news of Stillman who had stumbled into the Vale the day after Liv's capture, quite confused and upset about waking up in the woods with a nasty bump on his head but otherwise quite all right.

After the rebuilding came to an end, a grand celebratory feast, coupled with music and fireworks, was held in the garden.

Aaron and Chasmira sat together beneath one of the trees in the phoenix clearing. Aaron's hand crept towards Chasmira's subconsciously, and Chasmira's quite consciously acknowledged this fact by beginning to grow clammy, when Josh stumbled into the clearing, a wildly excited look flashing upon his face.

"Some totally hot fairy just showed up at the party, I mean, if *that's* how they make 'em in the past, you need to teach me how to time travel, Aaron. Anyways, says she wants to speak with you two, me, Sam, Hailey, Krystal, Tiff, Nathan, and Rachel in the phoenix clearing—well, heh, that'd be here."

Chasmira glanced curiously at Aaron who smiled, a hopeful knowing gleaming in his eyes. The others arrived quickly, casting questioning looks at him, but the next moment, the answer arrived.

Her footfall tread as silent as a still zephyr. The glistening, prismatic folds of her silky dress rippled behind her like the gentlest stream comprised of pure rainbows. From her fair skin and golden waves of hair emanated a natural sparkle, an angelic scintillation. The glitter also shone in the rosy highlights forming the most wonderfully natural crown upon her head. Most alluring of all though were her eyes, humble yet powerful, constantly varying their shades of blue, purple, and green.

"Greetings, Hero of 1,000 Years. *And* Heroes of Light, his helpers."

Josh's mouth fell open just a little lower at the sound of her song-like voice.

"Whoa, who *is* she?" he breathed almost reverently.

122

Rolling her eyes, Krystal fancied she noticed him drooling and elbowed him roughly. This did not affect him save that he stumbled, nearly crashing into Nathan who scowled.

"Heroes of Light? Us?" echoed Hailey, frowning. "But all of us did not help Aaron."

Amanda Danielle seemed to glow just a little bit brighter as a smile illuminated her face, and she replied, "Some of you helped in small ways, while others of you have not yet had your chance. However, I assure you that you will all play a part, in time. I assure you too that you should not be ashamed of how small your part may be, for even the smallest part can create the biggest alteration.

"But come. There are gifts I must bestow upon you all as the Heroes of Light, gifts I have been saving 'til I could restore the Destiny Stone to the Hero of 1,000 Years, when it might be safe for me to move about time and space once more. Come, let us all take hands..."

Everyone did so, Josh looking utterly disheartened that he did not get to hold Amanda Danielle's hand. He scowled at Nathan who clasped her hand just a little more tightly than necessary, lifting his head triumphantly. This small scene won unpleasant glares from both Rachel and Krystal, though neither boy took note.

Amanda Danielle breathed something ever so softly, and a soft zephyr slid over their skin, caressing each strand of their hair. Though gentle, the wind bore a strange sense of power. Then, the next moment, the garden vanished, and darkness enshrouded them.

"Welcome," Amanda Danielle's voice echoed in the dark. The immense blackness, while complete, did not feel ominous but peaceful, like sleeping.

With a clap of her hands, a sphere of white light hovered in their midst.

"Welcome," she repeated, smiling at their awed and curious faces, "to the Council Chamber of the fairies of Spectrum, whom I am proudly a part of. I bring you here because it is in this safe place that the gifts I bestow now have long been protected. Come."

They followed her by the glow of the orb to a triangular table made of an iridescent crystal; it emanated streams of prismatic light as the glitter of the white sphere bounced upon its surface. Upon the table and forming a perfect circle lay nine golden medallions.

As Amanda Danielle held up her hands, a glorious diamond sparkled upon one, five rings of various precious stones on the other.

"Heroes of Light, your task is done, for now. And you have done well. Soon our worlds and times shall depart. But first, I have gifts I wish to bestow upon you for your bravery, both past and future."

She slipped one of the rings onto each of the girls' fingers; the diamond she kept for herself.

"These are very precious stones and shall someday prove useful. Keep them always with you."

To each of them, she bestowed the golden medallions, each bearing the image of a white dove carrying a white lily. "These medallions bear my crest. Use them if you should ever have need to prove your allegiance to me, to the Fairy Council, or to anyone who serves the light.

"Now, I must return you to your own time and place. Come."

She cupped the light once more in her delicate fingers, and they followed her 'til its rays glittered upon a smooth lake. She paused at the shore, and they beside her, all watching calmly yet expectantly until, from beneath the curtain of blackness, the most enchanting ship emerged. It looked as though it was constructed of pure mother of pearl and was completely covered on every side by white lilies. Their petals unfurled wide, their sweet scent filling them all with a beautiful serenity.

Amanda Danielle bid them follow her as the ship stopped in perfect silence before them. They each boarded by means of a giant lily which served as a sort of elevator. And then, once all stood captivated upon deck, the fairy took the mother-of-pearl wheel and steered them with gentle hands away from the shore, into the darkness, which was no longer black in the ship's glistening, pure white sheen.

After several moments of silence and after the shore receded from their view, Amanda Danielle's song-like voice broke through the silent black. "We approach the time barrier. In only moments, you shall all find yourselves back in your own time and place."

"Thank you," said Aaron. "For all you've done for us."

A chorus of "thank-you's" rang out, and Amanda Danielle nodded, smiling sweetly. "Likewise, heroes. May Amiel bless you..."

As they vanished from her presence, her last words echoed, "Until we meet again."

* * *

Finally, the day dawned when all the Scintillates and Mira Liv had summoned must return to the past, including Liv herself.

As everyone gathered in the garden, she opened up a wide portal, a white light streaming through. As the fairies and elves climbed in, she, Taylor, and Dianne remained behind to say good-bye to Aaron and the others.

Dianne flew up to Aaron, dropping in his hand a small, blue, shining stone.

"It's a summons stone. Use it to call me if you ever need help. Even a thousand years can't separate our friendship...or something cheesy like that. I'll miss you anyways."

Aaron closed his hand around the stone and smiled. "Thanks."

Dianne nodded. "Well, nice meeting all of ya."

As she flitted into the portal, Aaron slipped the stone into his pocket.

"Yes, *very* nice," Taylor giggled, winking at him before slipping inside behind Dianne.

Then Liv walked up to them.

Aaron studied her eyes. Though they yet sparkled joyfully, contentedly, some of their lonely sorrow had already returned.

"Will—will you be all right?"

Liv smiled, beautifully yet sadly. "Just as Rorrim belonged in his own time, I belong in mine. The Mira tell me my cousins have returned to our wood, and I will feel lonely no more. I have been blessed to know such friends as you, Aaron Ruiz, Chasmira Eriz, Rachel Miner, Nathan Schmidt, but..." She gently placed their hands in one another's 'til they formed a small, connected arc. Her eyes sparkled tearfully. "This is where you belong—together, in your own time."

She started towards the portal but then turned, the white light enveloping her in an angelic glow. "Besides, not even a million years could really keep me away from you. You will always be in my heart."

Somehow, the words didn't sound cheesy as she spoke them. Rather, they sounded sweet, an echoing symbol of her future wisdom and brilliance as queen. As she stepped through the portal, she reserved her last glance for Aaron. Tears glittered down her soft cheeks, and the light illuminated the liquid spheres like tiny rainbows. A soft breeze blew her curls all about her like gentle streamers. Then the light swallowed her, and the portal closed in a flash.

All stood in pensive silence for some time before Mr. Root said quietly, "Well, let's all head back to school."

As everyone started back for the mansion, Chasmira noticed Aaron was uncommonly quiet and asked softly, "Are you okay?"

"Yeah...just thinking...

"You know, we never did find out who Rorrim's nephew was, the one supposedly trying to off me? I bet you anything it was Dristann..."

"Aaron," Chasmira sighed, "must we?"

Aaron shook his head. "Sorry. I guess it's really not all that important, now everyone is all right."

After another moment's silence, Rachel exclaimed, "Man, I *really* don't believe she just got me to touch your hand."

"Oh, *please*." Aaron rolled his eyes. "*I* don't believe *I* touched *yours*, the way you're always licking it—"

"I do *not always*—"

"You know," said Nathan, "this argument reminds me of this one book—"

"Oh, now, don't *you* start that," muttered Aaron, and everyone laughed as they entered the mansion.

Aaron paused to cast a last glance at the phoenix clearing. As Chasmira called to him, he followed her inside.

THE AMIELIAN LEGACY

The Stregoni Sequence *(Four-book collection)*

The Chronicles of the Mira

The Hero Chronicles *(Five-book collection)*

The Gailean Quartet *(Four-book collection)*

Loz *(Three-book collection)*

The Legends of Surprisers Series *(Three-book collection)*

The Pirates of Meleeon

The Crystal Rings

Bloodmaiden

Lily in the Snow and Other Elemental Tales

Chimes, La Mariposa: Two Tales of Emreal

The Last Star

StarChild

Follow Me

Black Lace

The Boy Who Fell From the Sky

Tears of a Vampire Prince: the First Krystine *(A companion to The Stregoni Sequence)*

Carousel in the Clouds

THE HERO CHRONICLES

THE HERO OF 1000 YEARS

HEROES REUNITED

HEROES OF THE DOVE

THE SECRET SISTER AND THE SILVER KNIGHT

THE PRINCESS OF DESTINY AND THE PRINCESS OF THE NIGHT